S0-BNF-432

What the press says about Harlequin Romances...

"...clean, wholesome fiction...always with an upbeat, happy ending."
—*San Francisco Chronicle*

"...a work of art."
—*The Globe & Mail*, Toronto

"Nothing quite like it has happened since *Gone With the Wind...*"
—*Los Angeles Times*

"...among the top ten..."
—*International Herald-Tribune*, Paris

"Women have come to trust these clean, easy-to-read love stories about contemporary people, set in exciting foreign places."
—*Best Sellers*, New York

Other titles by
ANNE HAMPSON
IN HARLEQUIN ROMANCES

1349—ETERNAL SUMMER
1388—UNWARY HEART
1420—PRECIOUS WAIF
1442—THE AUTOCRAT OF MELHURST
1467—BEYOND THE SWEET WATERS
1491—WHEN THE BOUGH BREAKS
1522—LOVE HATH AN ISLAND
1551—STARS OF SPRING
1570—HEAVEN IS HIGH
1595—GOLD IS THE SUNRISE
1622—THERE CAME A TYRANT
1646—ISLE OF THE RAINBOWS
1672—THE REBEL BRIDE
2082—CALL OF THE OUTBACK

Other titles by
ANNE HAMPSON
IN HARLEQUIN PRESENTS

108—PRIDE AND POWER
115—THE FAIR ISLAND
125—DEAR PLUTOCRAT
132—ENCHANTED DAWN
143—A MAN TO BE FEARED
152—AUTUMN TWILIGHT
168—DANGEROUS FRIENDSHIP
181—ISLE AT THE RAINBOW'S END
187—HILLS OF KALAMATA
196—FOLLOW A SHADOW

Many of these titles are available at your local bookseller,
or through the Harlequin Reader Service.

For a free catalogue listing all available Harlequin Romances,
send your name and address to:

HARLEQUIN READER SERVICE,
M.P.O. Box 707, Niagara Falls, N.Y. 14302
Canadian address: Stratford, Ontario, Canada N5A 6W4

or use order coupon at back of books.

Boss of Bali Creek

by

ANNE HAMPSON

Harlequin Books

TORONTO • LONDON • NEW YORK • AMSTERDAM • SYDNEY

Original hardcover edition published in 1973
by Mills & Boon Limited

ISBN 0-373-02099-6

Harlequin edition published September 1977

CHAPTER ONE

LORNA stood on the edge of the lawn and glanced with pride at the straight lines running along the grass. From the living-room window her aunt watched in some amusement and, turning, Lorna coloured a little.

'I just have to stand there and admire my handiwork,' she was saying deprecatingly a few moments later as, having stored away the mower in the shed, she entered the room in which Aunt Bertha sat, her knitting needles clicking. 'The lawn always looks so lovely when it's just been cut.'

Her aunt nodded; she had been rather preoccupied for the last few days, Lorna had noticed, and wondered what was on her mind.

'I don't really like your working in the garden every week-end like this. You should be resting, like anyone else who has a wage-earning job to do.'

'I love it.' Catching sight of her face in the mirror over the sideboard, Lorna gave a grimace. 'What a sight! How do I always manage to get my face smudged?'

Aunt Bertha merely shrugged abstractedly and laid down her knitting on her knee. She seemed a long way off and Lorna decided that this was a good time to go up and take a bath. Strange, she mused as she lay in the warm scented water, that Aunt Bertha should become thoughtful and preoccupied all at once. Plainly she had something on her mind, but Lorna would never dream of asking questions. When her aunt wished her to know what it was all about then she would tell her.

As she lay there, relaxed and drowsy with the heat, Lorna allowed her thoughts to wander retrospectively.

Jack . . . He had been so young and strong when first she met him; it did not seem possible at that time that he would be maimed, and would die so young. At eighteen she had fallen madly in love with him. He was her first boy-friend, handsome and much admired by all her friends; Lorna had been proud that he had chosen her, and a little supercilious, she recalled with a sudden frown. They hadn't been able to get married because Lorna's father withheld his consent, always maintaining that she and Jack weren't at all suited. Rebellious and angry, Lorna had quarrelled with her father, but her frustration had to remain, since even though she had left home she was still compelled to get her father's permission before she could marry. She and Jack had had to wait three years . . . and so much had happened in that time.

On reaching this stage in her retrospections Lorna tried to cut her thoughts and concentrate on her toilet, but without success. Wade Harcourt intruded unbidden. . . . Wade, who by rights should have been forgotten long ago, she told herself sternly as, enveloping her wet body in a towel, she went along the passage to her bedroom. It faced south, with a view on to the green hills of the tiny Dorset village where she lived with her aunt, who had given her a home on Jack's death six months ago. A widow with no children of her own, Bertha Gerrard had welcomed her niece's request that she come and live with her.

'I never thought Jack's brother would turn me out of the house,' wept Lorna, filled with distress at the idea of losing her little home. 'We only rented it, as you know, because of course Jack never earned any

6

money.' The house had belonged to Jack's brother and on their marriage Jack and Lorna had been grateful for the offer of it at a reasonable rent. But now Ivor had an eye to business and the house was to be put up for sale with vacant possession.

'It's a wicked thing to do,' Aunt Bertha had said angrily, but had added at once that she would be delighted to have Lorna come to live with her. If she got tired of having her, Lorna had said, she would look for somewhere else, eventually, when she had reorganized her life. But her aunt said she could stay permanently, so Lorna had moved her pathetic little store of possessions, and as she had a fairly well-paid post as a buyer in the fashion department of a large store, her life, after the first upheaval of moving and trying to readjust, had settled into smooth and rather pleasant lines. True, there was no excitement, but the freedom was enjoyable after the time she had had with Jack who, because of his condition, was invariably irritable with his wife.

'He doesn't know when he's well off!' Aunt Bertha would declare, glowering at him as he sat in his wheelchair. 'Anyone else would have put you in a home!'

'Shut up – and get out of here!'

'I don't know why she married you – being as you were, maimed for life—'

'Aunt Bertha ... please. . . .' Lorna's eyes would beseech; her hand would gesture towards the door. 'I'll come in and see you next Wednesday afternoon, but please go now.'

That was how it had been, for the three and a half years of her marriage, and despite her patience and compassion Lorna did at times feel that she had had just about enough of this life of slavery – working all day and coming home to see to the household chores as

7

well as caring for an invalid husband. She also felt that life was passing her by completely, and would continue to do so until she was quite old – too old to partake of the normal pleasures which were the lot of all her school friends, who were married, some with children, others waiting, so that they could both work to make more money for the home. They all pitied her, and one had gone so far as to say,

'How do you manage without sex, Lorna? I couldn't live the life you do. In fact, I'd never have married Jack, not after his accident, and his having his leg amputated and being paralysed and all that. I know it sounds selfish and hateful of me – but I'd have had to give him up.'

'He had no one, Sue. His brother's wife wouldn't have had him; she said he'd have to go into a home for the infirm if I didn't marry him—' Lorna had stopped then, realizing just what she had revealed. Without troubling herself about diplomacy her friend had said,

'So you did in fact toy with the idea of giving him up?'

Lorna had merely nodded then, refusing to carry the conversation further. For there had been a very good reason for her intention to give Jack up – and that reason had nothing at all to do with his infirmity.

'Lorna dear, tea's ready.' Aunt Bertha's voice brought Lorna's reflections to an end and she began rubbing herself down vigorously.

'I'll be there in a couple of minutes,' she called back. 'You can pour my tea; you know I don't care for it boiling hot.' She dropped the towel and began to dress, regarding herself in the long mirror as she did so.

Her figure hadn't altered since she was eighteen, she thought. It was still slender and shapely and rather at-

8

tractively curved. Four years since Wade Harcourt had said, his grey eyes tender and appreciative as he took her waist between his hands,

'I can span it without the least effort.' And he had lifted her right off her feet with the same ease. . . .

So tall he was, and good-looking, with the sort of lean and sinewed figure that instantly branded him a man of the outdoors. Boss of the huge Outback cattle station, Bali Creek, he had been over on a visit to his relatives. He and Lorna had met. 'You and I are meant for each other,' he had said. 'You didn't know your own mind at eighteen, my darling, but you're almost twenty-one now and you do know your own mind. Tell this Jack; he'll understand.'

'Lorna! What on earth are you doing up there?'

'Sorry, Auntie. I'm coming right away.'

The tea was daintily laid on a tray; this was set on a small table by the open french window, and the view was to the pretty garden with its immaculate lawn and shrubbery and its small bed of roses. Birds sang and the air was warm and fresh. Cattle grazed contentedly on the hillsides, and altogether it was a blissfully peaceful day in late spring, with the daffodils and narcissi in full bloom and green shoots abounding all over the place.

'You don't usually mess about so long with your appearance?' Aunt Bertha's gaze was a little curious as it rested on Lorna's face. 'What were you doing?'

Lorna gave a little gesture with her hand as she sat down.

'I was lost in thought, darling.'

Aunt Bertha frowned on hearing this.

'Not of the past? But what else could you be thinking of? It's time you put the whole unhappy business from you, Lorna, and began all over again.'

Lorna looked swiftly at her. There *was* something

9

strange about her; that tone, for instance, as she advised her niece to begin all over again. . . .

'How does one begin all over again, Auntie?'

To Lorna's surprise her aunt merely picked up a plate of sandwiches and handed it to her. But after a while she said, right out of the blue,

'How would you like a trip to Australia? I'm thinking of visiting Wade.'

Silence followed; Lorna felt the colour leave her face.

'I don't understand,' she said presently. 'I didn't know you had the money to take a trip to Australia?'

'I've had a win on the Premium Bonds,' her aunt calmly responded, pouring herself more tea.

'A win? When was this? You never mentioned it.'

'Last month. And I've been wondering what to do with it — Oh, I know I could put it away for a rainy day, but how dull and unimaginative, don't you think? I decided to write to Wade and see if he'd have us for a spell.' Aunt Bertha stopped, and there was no mistaking the frown that had settled on her brow. 'He — he was more than willing to have us.'

Lorna said, her soft and pleasant voice edged with a sudden huskiness,

'You go, by all means, Auntie, but it's quite impossible for me to accompany you. I have my job to think of. Besides, we couldn't leave this house, and the garden.' She shook her head, acutely aware of the wild beating of her heart. How could the mention of Wade by her aunt set her heart racing . . . after four long years? Wade, whose anger at her decision not to desert Jack in his affliction had been terrifying to witness. And after it had died he had adopted an air of arrogant indifference and his parting words had been,

'Go your own obstinate way! And as for me — I

10

never want to set eyes on you again as long as I live. Thank God there's a few thousand miles to separate us!'

So hurt he had been. Lorna had been left trembling and weeping, but never had she failed to understand that Wade too had suffered. He would be thirty-three now, she realized, and wondered if he had changed at all. Perhaps he was even leaner and tougher after a further four years of demanding Outback husbandry. He owned over ten thousand square miles of that hostile terrain, an inheritance that had been passed down from father to son over four generations.

'I can't go on my own, Lorna. You know very well how scared I am of flying. Why, I was petrified just going to Jersey, so it's impossible for me to fly all that way alone.'

Lorna looked suspiciously at her. She hadn't remembered any particular terror on the flight to Jersey late last year when, immediately after Jack's death, Aunt Bertha had insisted on taking Lorna away for a holiday.

'You could sail, then.'

'It takes too long.' Aunt Bertha shook her head. 'No, you must come with me.'

Reaching for her cup, Lorna took a drink. No use pretending she was unaware of what her aunt had in mind.

'Wade isn't married, obviously,' she murmured, speaking her thoughts aloud, 'otherwise you wouldn't be contemplating this trip.'

'I see you have the picture so it's no use my trying to disguise my motives. There's no reason at all, Lorna, why you two shouldn't get together now that you're free of that dreadful burden which I and everyone else, including your dear father – may he rest in peace –

11

considered you should never have taken upon yourself. Not one girl in a million would have married a man who could provide her with neither comfort nor companionship—'

'I couldn't desert him,' interrupted Lorna with a frown of impatience at her aunt's bringing up of the matter.

'Well, whether you were right or wrong in taking heed of your conscience it's all in the past now, thank heaven. As you know, I was responsible for your meeting Wade in the first place and ever since he left in such an angry mood I've blamed myself for causing misery to you both.'

'Then you shouldn't,' put in Lorna swiftly and indignantly. 'You were in no way to blame. Wade was visiting his cousin, Mrs. Frith, when we happened to call, and that's how we met. It's absurd for you to blame yourself.'

'Mrs. Frith was my friend. I asked you to take me there, in the sweet little car you then owned. Had I not been so stingy, and hired a taxi, it would never have happened.'

Lorna had to smile in spite of her rather confused feelings at the moment.

'How you do twist things around, darling! I shan't listen to such nonsense!'

Aunt Bertha lapsed into thought for a space and then,

'To get back to our trip to Wade's ranch– or station as they call their farms out there. I wrote, as I said—'

'I didn't think you knew Wade well enough to be on writing terms with him. Have you been corresponding all this time?'

'No, dear. I wrote only after I'd had my win. I asked him if he was married yet and in his reply he said no; I also said that you were now free, as Jack had died some months ago.'

'You did? But how pointed your letter must have seemed to him!' Lorna coloured delicately, the rosy hue adding enchantment to her finely-etched features, features framed by a glorious mass of pale gold hair, long, and straight but for the ends, which flicked up in the most charming way. Her violet eyes were bright with indignation at the idea of her aunt's wording her letter in so blunt a way that what she had in mind must immediately have made itself transparently obvious to him. 'Really, Auntie, you ought not to have written a letter like that!'

'Like what, Lorna?' Aunt Bertha flicked her hands. 'What was wrong in my asking if we could come and pay him a visit? He got on all right with me, and he fell in love with you. He'll be delighted to see us.'

'Fell in love. . . .' Lorna knew she was pale now, the colour having swiftly receded from her cheeks. 'He hated me when he left.'

'You never told me the whole,' said Aunt Bertha after a moment's pause. 'You merely said he had asked you to give Jack up and marry him instead. I've always been curious to know what really happened.' Her tone and wording were an invitation, and after a slight hesitation Lorna related all there was to relate.

'We met at Mrs. Frith's, as you know. While you and she were in the kitchen getting the refreshments we began talking. I had on my engagement ring and he kept on staring at it. It was love at first sight with us both, Auntie, we knew it. For some time, though, I had been having doubts about the relationship existing between Jack and me. I knew that the head-over-heels thing I had experienced on first getting to know him was merely calf-love, the sort of thing many an eighteen-year-old experiences. Our relationship during the

13

years we'd had to wait had grown into something almost dull. I often felt that Father was right when he so strongly affirmed we weren't suited. I did in fact periodically suggest to Jack that we part, but he would then become sentimental—' Lorna broke off, blushing again and her aunt nodded understandingly.

'You'd have a highly emotional making up, as it were?'

'That's right. And then I'd feel I was being silly, and that it was the waiting which was becoming a strain. Jack used to say this and assured me I'd feel differently once we were married.'

'I understand. These makings-up can be pretty wonderful when you're really in love. I know, because I used to quarrel with David on purpose so that I could bring one about.'

Lorna smiled, as she was expected to, but she was in no mood for humour, with the first meeting with Wade Harcourt so vividly occupying her thoughts. Almost instantly on being introduced to him she had felt her heartbeats increase in the most exciting way. Her body had seemed to quiver from head to foot as delicious tingles ran the length of her spine. She had been shy and tongue-tied, she recalled, and Wade had seemed to be highly amused by his ability to throw her into such confusion. His laugh had sent her pulses racing, the touch of his hand as he deliberately made contact – for no reason that was in any way apparent – was even at that time enough to make her wish for more . . . for the feel of his lips on hers, the proximity of that hard body. . . .

Swiftly Lorna checked her outspreading thoughts and said,

'Wade insisted I meet him; he took me out to dinner and afterwards we danced. I felt so dreadfully guilty,

14

I remember,' she continued reflectively. 'I was so enjoying myself with Wade, and yet I was conscious all the time of my engagement to Jack. I'd taken off my ring and that made me feel worse.' She paused and her aunt remarked,

'Consciences can be a darned nuisance. But do go on, dear.'

'Wade was terribly – well – bossy, and wouldn't listen when I said I mustn't ever see him again. So I agreed to do so and we saw each other all the time. And it was as if fate were helping for Jack had to go to Glasgow for his firm and there was then no check on our meeting regularly. I even stayed off work for a couple of days so that we could have a few trips out in the car Wade had hired. I took him to Cheddar Gorge on one of the days and to Bournemouth on the other. We seemed, quite suddenly, to have known each other a long, long time, Auntie. It was most peculiar . . . sort of uncanny.'

'No such thing. You were in love, you were suited. This was very far from being uncanny. It was the most natural – and beautiful – thing in the world. Love is, Lorna, real love.'

Tears gathered in Lorna's eyes, but she blinked them away before her aunt should notice.

'Wade was now quite possessive and he told me to be honest with Jack and then give him back his ring. This I intended doing, just as soon as he returned.' Lorna broke off, emotion choking back the words she was ready to utter. 'He – he had the accident, as – as you know, and I was sent for to go to the hospital, as at that time his brother was abroad, on holiday. I was so filled with pity, Aunt Bertha—' Lorna stopped again, trying to collect herself. 'It was a terrible decision to have to make,' she whispered. 'I loved Wade dearly – oh, with

15

all my heart I loved him – but Jack needed me.' She spread her hands. 'You know the rest. His brother and his wife came home; Kathleen without hesitation said she would definitely not have an invalid in her house, making demands on her time, so I made my decision. . . .'

For a while silence ensued after Lorna had finished speaking. Her aunt's mouth was tight. She had personally tried to dissuade her niece from taking on the burden of a man who could never hope to earn a penny in his life, who could give her nothing but worry and hard work. As things had turned out he had also given her heartache in plenty, since he had no such word as gratitude in his vocabulary; all was taken for granted after the first few weeks. He did not mind at all that his wife was going out to work to keep him; he became so irritable that he scarcely spoke a civil word to her, and never had Aunt Bertha heard him say a thank you when Lorna had handed him a cup of tea or brought him in his cigarettes or favourite brand of sweets. Lorna herself had gone without clothes, without pleasure of any kind at all. In the three and a half years she had been married to him she had never taken a holiday, or even a day trip anywhere.

The pneumonia that had killed him was a blessing, thought Aunt Bertha grimly, although of course she naturally kept this from her niece who, on being told there was no hope, as Jack's lungs were already weakened by his condition, said with deep regret in her voice,

'So young. . . . Isn't it awful, Aunt Bertha, to think that he's going to die?'

Yes, thought Aunt Bertha now as she glanced at her niece across the table, that pneumonia had indeed been a blessing.

16

'There's no need for me to ask if you still care for Wade,' she said. 'I've seen it in your eyes all along: the anguish, the regret for what might have been. You asked just now how does one start all over again. This win of mine has made it possible for you to go over and see Wade—'

'It's kind of you, Auntie, but I can't just go over to Australia and throw myself at him. I've just told you, Wade hated me when he left.'

'Did he say so?'

'Not in so many words, but I could see it in his face.'

'Rubbish! A man doesn't love one moment and hate the next.'

'He did say he never wished to see me again as long as he lived.'

'A natural reaction to your obstinacy. A man like Wade is used to having his wishes and instructions carried out. He had told you to give Jack up and you refused. Wade knew – as we all did – that you were wrong in following the dictates of your conscience; by your adamant attitude you were ruining his life as well as your own and it was understandable that he should be angry, and, in his anger, that he should say things he didn't mean.'

'He was very bitter,' murmured Lorna almost to herself. And then, emphatically, and a little urgently because to her surprise she was beginning to weaken, 'I can't go, Auntie. It would be impossible to pick up the threads after all this time.'

'I'm not suggesting you could pick up the threads. But I am saying that you can start again.'

Start again. . . . The temptation to see Wade again was taking root, and growing. What harm could there be in making an effort? – in going over, and seeing just

17

how he would react on meeting her, in the knowledge that she was now free?

'What exactly did he say in his letter, Auntie? You said he was more than willing to have us.'

'That's right. He seemed quite enthusiastic, in fact.' Aunt Bertha appeared to become more than a little interested in the mundane matter of stirring her tea; this she did vigorously, and for far longer than was necessary.

'His letter,' began Lorna hesitantly, 'can I read it? If you don't want me to,' she went on to add hastily, 'it's all right, but—'

'You could have read it, dear, but I'm afraid I've thrown it away. You know how I detest keeping things around.'

'Auntie,' exclaimed Lorna almost before she had finished speaking, 'you're the world's most avid hoarder of letters! – and you know it!'

'I've changed, dear. I do destroy them now. About Wade's – it was just an ordinary one. The obvious reply to mine. He said how nice it was to hear from me – or words to that effect. And then he went on to say that of course we must come over, if we wished. And we could stay as long as we liked.'

'He didn't – mention – me?'

'But of course he did. He said he was very much looking forward to seeing you again.' Absent-mindedly Aunt Bertha put more sugar in her tea and began stirring it again, staring hard at the little whirlpool she made.

'He did?' Lorna found her heart beating just a little faster.

'Are you coming with me?' her aunt asked, ignoring these two small words.

A long pause followed before Lorna said,

18

'I don't know, Auntie. It – it would be wonderful to see him again, though.'

'I've been talking to Mrs. Southerby about the trip, and she's promised to look after the house – just come in now and then to put the heat on if necessary. Mr. Mitchell will be only too glad to do the garden – he's been finding it a bit hard going since he retired, you know, so the extra money will come in handy.'

Lorna stared.

'You seem to have everything arranged already. How could you be so sure I'd agree to come with you?'

'I wasn't sure,' her aunt admitted, 'but I was optimistic. You're a sensible girl, and as the sensible thing is to try and make something of your life, I felt you would at least give the matter some serious consideration.' She paused a moment. 'You are coming with me, aren't you, Lorna?'

A small hesitation as Lorna tried to visualize the meeting between Wade and herself. As she had said, he had been angry and bitter on leaving her. But that was four years ago. Time must surely have taken the edge from his anger, and gone a long way to dissolving his bitterness. He had written in his letter to her aunt that he was looking forward to seeing her again . . . surely that was a sign that he had forgiven her. She looked across at her aunt and said at last,

'Yes, I'm coming with you.'

Aunt Bertha wasted no time at all, and within a fortnight of Lorna's agreeing to go to Australia with her they were on the plane.

'What a rush!' Lorna had gasped a couple of days previously on their returning home from a shopping spree in Bristol. 'Really, Auntie, I didn't know you had

19

it in you to dash about all over the place like this!'

'I've never had the means to dash about for anything. What a joy money is! No, you needn't ask me again how much I won, because I shan't tell you. All I will say is that it was one of the bigger prizes!'

'Obviously it was,' laughed Lorna, who seemed to have grown years younger during the past week. She had told her boss of her aunt's projected trip and he had agreed to find a replacement for Lorna until she returned. He naturally wanted to know how long she would be away, but this she could not tell him. If by some miracle Wade still loved her, she thought, she would not be returning at all.

If by some miracle Wade still loved her. ... This thought came to her again as she looked down at the dwindling coastline. What a delicious sensation it was to dream of a future – a whole long, long future – with Wade.

'I wonder what Bali Creek is like.' She spoke her thoughts aloud and saw her aunt smile.

'What a tonic it is to see you so happy! I'm rather enjoying the role of fairy godmother.'

'You've been wonderful, Auntie. I hated the idea of accepting so much, but you've bullied me into having lots of lovely clothes, and the most expensive hair-do I've ever had.'

'You've never had any sort of hair-do for years,' Aunt Bertha could not resist retorting grimly. 'Your hard-earned money was always spoken for before you received it!'

Lorna naturally allowed that to pass without comment.

'And the shoes! What a lot of shoes I now own!'

'About time. I did like those sandals, though, Lorna. Made in Italy – but they do make beautiful footwear

20

there.'

'The cocktail dresses,' mused Lorna, 'I wonder if I'll really need them?'

'They're there if you do. And if you don't they'll not eat anything.'

'They make their own amusements on these cattle stations. They have barn dances and film shows and parties. I've been reading up about the life in the Outback, and on the whole it seems to be rather tough.'

Her aunt looked a trifle anxious.

'I hope you're going to enjoy it, dear?'

'Enjoy it? I'll love it! You know very well how I prefer anything close to nature – and the life on an Australian cattle station is very close to nature from what I can gather. There is solitude and silence, and clean fresh air and wide open spaces.' Lorna felt almost lighthearted with all the excitement, which was made more stimulating by its contrast with the dull routine of those three and a half years spent with Jack. Her aunt, who at sixty-four had always seemed rather old to Lorna, had during the past fortnight bustled about like a woman half her age. Money was for spending, she said, and spend she did! Everything she and Lorna were taking with them in the way of clothes was brand new; so were their suitcases and handbags. Aunt Bertha had even had a manicure to go with her hair-do, and a facial which, she admitted with a sort of disgusted humour, had made not the slightest difference to her 'lines and bags'.

'These advertisements are fraudulent,' she had declared. 'I'd sue them if I wasn't going away!'

'I wonder what Bali Creek is like,' Lorna was saying again many hours after they had boarded the plane. 'Wade used to say I'd love the house. . . .' She tailed off as memory surged in, and the rest was kept to herself.

21

She would be the fourth bride of Bali Creek, he had said. And he had added, his soft Australian voice filled with tender emotion, 'You'll be the most beautiful of them all . . . and the best loved.'

'With Wade's great wealth,' said Aunt Bertha in response to Lorna's speculative inquiry, 'his house should be something special. Of course, these Outback graziers spend most of their time out of doors, but I should imagine Wade would look to the home comforts for all that.'

'I shall soon know, anyway.' She felt a sudden quickening of her heartbeats. The meeting . . .? Surely it must have an element of awkwardness about it, for both of them. The parting had been wrathful on Wade's part, tearful and contrite on hers. She had gone back on her word, after promising him faithfully that she would break with Jack and marry him before he returned to Australia. So happy he had been on extracting that promise from her; he had seemed much younger than his twenty-nine years in spite of the little tinges of grey at his temples and the fanned-out lines at the corner of his eyes, the result of having continually to narrow them against the fierce Australian sun. What a surprise everyone would have, he had laughed, when he brought back his wife, after having been in England a mere five weeks. Putting the memory from her, Lorna spoke to her aunt.

'I'll be glad when the first few minutes are over.'

'You're not worried about the first encounter with Wade? You mustn't, dear. Haven't I told you he's looking forward to seeing you?'

Lorna smiled and nodded.

'Yes, Auntie. Nevertheless, I've got butterflies in my tummy!'

When eventually they landed there was then a long

journey through the Great Divide and later through a terrain of sub-tropical vegetation such as low eucalypts and brigalow scrub, and finally across a landscape alternating between bushy acacia and vast stretches of temperate grassland. On reaching their destination they were met by one of Wade's employees, Stuart Clarke, who had brought the overlanding car from Bali Creek the previous day. After the introductions and a few polite questions and answers regarding the journey up till now they were in the car and driving away from the railway station. They would be spending one night under canvas, Stuart told them, this owing to the great distance they had to travel before reaching the Bali Creek homestead, which was in the Northern Territory.

'We shall arrive there about lunch time tomorrow,' he said. 'The Boss has been away in Alice Springs, but he'll be home by then, so he'll be there to welcome you.'

CHAPTER TWO

On the second day, after driving through miles and miles of Bali Creek terrain, where cattle grazed and stockriders could now and then be seen silhouetted against a blue metallic sky, Stuart at last pointed to little wooded region just coming into view beyond a small hill.

'The homestead,' he said briefly, and automatically increased his speed. He had had enough of driving for a while; Lorna deduced this by his tone, and by the way he had once or twice stifled a yawn. His eyes were sun-tired, his brow moist with the heat.

The homestead. ... As they approached it more closely Lorna saw that it had a mellowed aspect, with climbers giving a delightful display of colour to some of its walls. It was a straggling building, a manor house of charm and character that had gracefully and unobtrusively absorbed all additions which its occupiers had considered it necessary to make throughout the hundred and twenty years it had stood in the elegant solitude of its surrounding landscaped gardens. Weathered walls sported the bright blossoms of bougainvilleas and other exotic trailing plants. Poinsettias, those flaming beauties whose scarlet leaves formed haloes round their inconspicuous flowers, were providing splashes of colour everywhere. Palms and casuarinas and eucalypts formed the wooded enclosure which sheltered the homestead from wind and sun. To the west rose the clear outline of the Macdonnell Ranges, while to the north of the homestead, and some distance from it, lay the bungalows of the stockriders and other people employed by Wade. Lorna was soon to learn that a sort of manorial system existed on many of the Outback stations. The Bali Creek Station was a community of this description, supporting a great many families whose housing was free. Things like vegetables and milk were also there for the taking; there was a school and shop, there were facilities for recreation and free transport into the nearest town whenever anyone wanted to buy commodities not obtainable in the 'village' shop. A doctor, widowed and retired, had called one day two years ago when he was on a sightseeing tour of the Outback. He had stayed a week, gone home and packed his belongings, and returned to take possession of the bungalow offered to him by Wade. He was now semi-retired!

'So here we are at last!' Aunt Bertha stretched and yawned on getting out of the car. 'A bath and bed is all I want just now.'

Lorna had also left the car; she was conscious of Stuart's voice saying he would drive round to the back, where the luggage would be unloaded and taken into the house. But her whole mind and vision were occupied by the tall slim giant who, having taken the verandah steps with the agility of a ten-year-old, was now covering the small distance separating him from his visitors. Lorna discovered she was trembling, and that her nerves fluttered, out of control. He had changed, was her first and rather disappointed conclusion. His added years seemed to have brought a harshness to his features which, she recalled, were always rather stern – but no more than that. His mouth seemed thinner, his grey eyes sharper and more penetrating. The fan lines were more numerous, the high cheekbones below them so prominent that they seemed to have no covering of flesh at all, just skin, dark sun-

25

bitten skin, tough and faintly shining. His eyebrows were dark and straight, his hair still thick and healthy, its deep brown colour unchanged but for an added touch of grey to the already lighter shade at his temples.

'Wade. ...' The whispered name escaped her unbidden. Within her nothing had changed, she realized with wonderment. She could have melted unselfconsciously into his arms and lifted her face to invite his kiss. No, nothing within her had changed, despite the surface change in Wade. 'It's so very nice to see you again.' Eagerly she extended a hand; it was taken in Wade's strong brown one ... but no responding smile appeared to soften the harshness of his face. She stared, bewildered, as, withdrawing his hand almost immediately, he turned to her aunt.

'I trust you had a fairly pleasant journey, Mrs. Gerrard?'

'All very comfortable – and exciting!' she returned enthusiastically, and brightly, considering her tiredness and her declaration of a moment ago that all she wished for was a bath and a bed. 'It was so good of you to agree to have us, Wade – you don't mind my calling you Wade? Mr. Harcourt sounds so formal.'

'Call me Wade by all means. And now, you must come in and have something to eat and drink. You must be needing refreshments?' As yet he had spoken no word at all to Lorna, and she felt a flatness slowly creeping over her. 'One of the lubras is ready to show you your rooms, which I trust you'll like.'

'We're sure to,' from Lorna, who was suddenly determined to make him speak to her. He turned and looked down into her clear violet eyes, taking in their expression of bewilderment and frowning slightly as if at some secret thought. Lorna wondered what he was

26

thinking; she tried to decide whether during this pro-longed unsmiling stare he was taking in the changes which had inevitably affected her own appearance, then saw to her surprise and embarrassment that he was merely looking indifferently through her in a pre-occupied kind of way.

'How are you getting on these days, Lorna?' he in-quired at last with the cool politeness he would extend to any visitor to his home. 'Your aunt told me of your bereavement. I'm sorry to hear about it.' No emotion in his voice or glance. It seemed quite impossible that he had ever held her in those strong arms, had let her feel the hard possessiveness of his mouth on hers.

'I'm getting along fine, thank you, Wade.' Suddenly she wanted to get away, for this was not the attitude of a man who, so Aunt Bertha had maintained, had writ-ten to say he was very much looking forward to seeing her again. A dusky girl was standing on the verandah in an attitude of waiting and swiftly Lorna said, 'Is the girl waiting for me?'

Turning, Wade nodded and said yes, Dinah was waiting to show her and her aunt to their rooms.

'I'll go then, if you don't mind?' She glanced awk-wardly at him and without affording him time to answer she left him and her aunt together and joined Dinah, who took her through a beautifully appointed sitting-room into a high-ceilinged hall and then up a wide curving staircase to a bedroom overlooking the front garden.

'Is there anything you want, miss?' asked the girl with a smile.

'My suitcases?'

'They are in the dressing-room. I will unpack them for you if you wish?'

Lorna shook her head, glancing at a closed door.

27

'No, thank you; I'll do it myself.'

When the girl had gone Lorna went over and opened the door. Her suitcases were on a large oaken stool and after a swift glance around, taking in the huge wardrobe and dressing-table, she picked up one of her cases and carried it into the bedroom, placing it on the bed and snapping open the locks. Her eyes were filmed with tears and she straightened up even as she had begun to take things from the case. She was doing this automatically, she realized, doing it to try and take her mind off the distinctly cold reception she had received from Wade. She thought of the abrupt way she had left him – not the way to treat one's host on first arriving at his house – and wondered if he had noticed her haste to get away from him.

'I shouldn't have come,' she quivered, discovering she was cold and that her hands and forehead were clammy. She felt she had all the symptoms of influenza, but knew it was a mental thing with which she was affected, not a physical one. 'No, I shouldn't have come.'

The window was wide open and the pretty curtains were billowing into the room. With the intention of closing the window a little she stopped just before she reached it. She was right above the spot where they had all been standing, she noticed, and down there Wade and Aunt Bertha were still talking.

'—no matter what you say, Wade, I do think you could have been a little kinder to her.'

'Mrs. Gerrard, you seem to forget that I told you not to bring her.' The voice was edged with impatience and with censure. 'You wrote asking me if I would have you as my guest – after having explained that you'd won some money and wished to travel to Australia. You mentioned that Lorna was living with you, as she

28

was now a widow, and asked if she could come too. I wrote in very plain words, Mrs. Gerrard, that while you yourself would be most welcome, I had decided after some thought that I did not want Lorna here as my guest. In your next letter you accepted this, but just before you left England you wrote again saying you would have to bring Lorna as you couldn't leave her alone in the house—'

'It's in such a lonely spot, Wade.'

'That's no concern of mine, Mrs. Gerrard. I had no time to reply to that last letter – you intended it to be that way, obviously. Had I had time to reply I should have told you definitely that Lorna was not welcome here.'

White to the lips, Lorna stepped back, but her legs felt weak and she stopped again, brushing trembling fingers across her forehead. It was damp still, but suddenly a pain shot through it, affecting the backs of her eyes, and the tears were released.

'I do understand how you feel.' Her aunt's words still reached Lorna clearly and she tried to move further away from the window, but her legs refused to function. 'Lorna hurt you dreadfully—'

'She threw me over, Mrs. Gerrard, after making me a solemn promise that she would marry me.' So harsh the tones, but there was no real bitterness in them. Lorna knew instinctively that Wade had long since recovered from the hurt he had sustained at her hands.

'It's in the past, Wade,' persuasively from Aunt Bertha, whose object was so transparently revealed now. Deliberately she had told fibs in order to convince her niece that she would be welcome at Bali Creek. 'You loved her once—'

'Once, yes.'

'You could begin again.' Listening, Lorna went hot

29

all over. Why didn't Aunt Bertha accept the truth and let the matter drop!

'I could *not* begin again! For one thing I haven't the least desire to do so, and for another . . . for another, Mrs. Gerrard, I'm now engaged to someone else.'

Engaged. . . . Lorna did now manage to move, over to the bed where, with a mechanical movement, she closed the lid of her suitcase and placed it on the floor. She lay down after taking off her shoes, pressing her aching brow against the cool linen of the coverlet. Her tears fell unrestrainedly for a few moments, until she realized she was marking the beautifully-starched bed-cover. She rose then, despising herself for her weakness, and, determined to rally from the blow that had shattered all her happy dreams of a reunion with Wade, she went and took a bath and then changed into one of her prettiest dresses. It was of figured cotton, bought especially for the hot climate. Its crisp newness and bright colour helped to lift her spirits somewhat; the application of a little make-up to her cheeks and lips helped even further, and by the time she went to join Wade and Aunt Bertha for lunch she had regained much of her composure.

She was glad she had overheard what Wade had to say, as now she was warned. There would be no danger of her becoming over-friendly towards him, no possibility of her allowing him to make a guess at her feelings. Lorna would of course have liked to leave Bali Creek at once, but as that was impossible she must adopt an attitude towards Wade similar to that which he adopted towards her. As for Aunt Bertha – much as she deplored her methods and her scheming, Lorna admitted that her intentions were good, and therefore decided she must never know the unhappiness she had brought to her niece by insisting she accompany her to

30

Australia. Lorna decided also that the simplest way to put her aunt at complete ease was for her, Lorna, to say that now she had met Wade again all she ever felt for him was gone.

Gone! How difficult it would be to voice that lie. But Lorna resolved to do so, since then her aunt would have no need for self-reproach and could without hindrance thoroughly enjoy her holiday. Perhaps she would not want to stay too long, now that her plan had gone all awry. Lorna sincerely hoped her aunt would not want to remain at Bali Creek more than a month at the most, since this was quite long enough for Lorna to endure the strain of seeing Wade every day and having to act as if he meant no more to her than any other man on the station.

'Your aunt is resting,' Wade informed Lorna immediately on her entering the dining-room where a most appetizing lunch was to be served. 'I've sent her up some sandwiches and a pot of tea.' Cool the drawl and faintly clipped. Wade politely pulled out a chair for Lorna, who thanked him stiffly but with a smile. She was remembering those occasions when she and Wade had eaten together, in the little Tudor inns of Dorset, eaten in the intimacy of shaded lights and cosy log fires, and something like a knife seemed to turn in her heart so that the pain she felt was physical.

'The long journey was a little trying for her. She'll be all right when she's had a sleep.'

Wade wasn't listening. Beside his place he had some papers and it was on these that his attention rested. Lorna was served with soup, but she soon found that delicious as it was she had no appetite for it.

'Is something wrong?' He was all concern for his guest on noticing her put down her spoon and lean back in her chair.

31

Lorna shook her head.

'No, it's very tasty. I just don't feel hungry, that's all.' She felt awkward, and an intruder, aware as she was of being an unwelcome guest in his house.

'Would you care for something different? Grapefruit? Prawn cocktail?'

Again she shook her head.

'No, thank you, Wade. I'll have some steak if I may, and perhaps a few vegetables.' Her voice lacked confidence; she had no stomach for anything at all but felt he would insist that she had something.

Perhaps he sensed her discomfiture, and if so he would be honest enough to admit to being to blame. This appeared to be the case, for from then on he gave her his attention, laying aside the papers he had been perusing.

'How long are you and your aunt thinking of staying?' he inquired politely after ten minutes or so of casual conversation.

'I've no idea how long Auntie wants to stay.' Across the table she looked at him . . . so severe his features, and so firm his mouth and jaw. A product of hard outdoor living, she thought, a man of perfect health and fitness. 'I – we don't want to inconvenience you, Wade, so you must tell us when the time comes that we're overstaying our welcome.' Did he give a slight start on hearing this? wondered Lorna, half wishing she had not said it. After all, they had only just arrived, so it was hardly what he would have expected to hear.

'We usually allow our visitors to decide for themselves how long they'll stay.'

'We?' The one small word was out before Lorna gave herself time to check it. She was of course thinking about his fiancée – although why she should she could not have explained. His fiancée could not possibly be

32

included in the 'we', simply because she was not living here.

'Graziers in general. Visitors are welcome on these stations; they come all the time – tourists wanting a night's accommodation, a rest from driving or camping out. Others come because they're interested in the way we live, others because they're moving from one part of the country to another.'

'I see.' Lorna toyed with her meat. 'You have no other guests at present, though?'

'Not at present, no. In a fortnight's time we have two students from the agricultural college just outside Brisbane. We have them periodically; they come to find out how their theory lines up with practice.' There was a faint sneer in his voice, she thought, and supposed he and his kind were a trifle supercilious towards those who theorize without first getting down to the practicalities of their subject.

'Are they men?' asked Lorna, but hoping they might be women – or girls, rather, who would perhaps be company for her.

'Yes, they're men. We do have female students, quite often,' he added, his eyes on her face, which she knew was pale but which, she hoped, portrayed no sign of her unhappiness.

'It must be an interesting occupation.' They were idly talking, just to pass the time; strangers almost, thought Lorna, allowing her eyes to wander round the elegant room. The fourth bride of Bali Creek, Wade had said, so tenderly. She would be the most beautiful, and the best loved of them all. Her mind leapt on a little, to the heartbreaking choice she made, a sacrifice that robbed her and Wade of what might have been. Then this trip . . . hope had burst upon her as Aunt Bertha spoke about it, asking Lorna to accompany her.

33

Yes, hope had filled her heart, only to be cruelly torn away within minutes of her arrival here. Wade was engaged to be married. . . . There was no place at Bali Creek for the girl he had once loved.

Her reflections had the effect of making her lips tremble and to her surprise Wade said,

'Are you quite well, Lorna? You're so pale, and you seem – distressed in some way?'

What must she return to these questions? Evasion was essential, for he must never guess the truth. His love had died; he should not ever learn that hers had lived, and flourished all this time.

'I haven't been entirely myself since Jack died,' she said at last, and that was of course the truth. The strain of the long thankless years had seemed to increase on her husband's death. Reaction, the doctor had said when at last she was persuaded by her aunt to 'go and see about those nerves'.

'It's only six months, your aunt told me?' Terse the voice and narrowed the eyes. Wade reached for a silver dish and helped himself to salad from it.

'That's right.' She paused a moment, watching him. She just had to change the subject and she said the first thing that came into her head. 'You grow all this yourself?'

Wade looked swiftly at her, his brow knitted in a frown. He seemed puzzled and surprised by this irrelevant question, as well he might, she owned, her face softly pink now, under his curious scrutiny.

'We're practically self-supporting here, yes,' he answered at length, his gaze still on her, taking in the sudden touch of colour, the long thick eyelashes lowered to hide her expression. 'We have to be, since the nearest town is seventy-two miles away.'

'So far as that? I knew of course that the cattle

34

stations themselves were long distances from each other.'

'My nearest neighbour lives just over a hundred miles away, at Blue River Downs.' He was thoughtful all at once and Lorna knew instinctively that Blue River Downs was the home of his fiancée. She said, as if compelled by a force beyond her control,

'The owners . . . they're friends of yours?'

He hesitated.

'I'm enaged to the owner's daughter,' he said, and looked straight at Lorna who, after a long quivering sigh she could not hold back, managed to say,

'Engaged . . . how nice. I'm – I'm glad for y-you, Wade.'

'Thank you.'

Lorna swallowed convulsively.

'Is the wedding to be soon?'

'Fairly soon.'

Impelled again by something beyond her control Lorna asked what his fiancée was like.

'Is she dark or fair?'

Wade seemed amused by her interest, a circumstance that hurt beyond all reason.

'She's as dark as you are fair.'

'Dark . . .' Strangely, Lorna hadn't expected him to fall in love with anyone dark.

'Her hair is black, her eyes brown—' He stopped suddenly and actually laughed. 'You don't really want to know any more, do you, Lorna? I mean, you can't be that interested in the girl I'm going to marry?'

She coloured delicately, toying again with the meat on her plate.

'No – I'm sorry. It was just idle curiosity.'

'You'll be meeting Olga and her parents quite soon,' he then told her casually. 'They're coming to spend a

35

couple of days at Bali Creek. There'll be a few others also; I'm giving a party and the following evening a film show. We make our own amusements here, but I expect you know that?'

Lorna nodded her head.

'Yes, I do know.' Boring, unimportant conversation, thought Lorna dejectedly, unable to help recalling how, during those idyllic days of their whirlwind courtship, there hadn't been time for all the things they wished to say to one another.

'We'll make up when I get you to Bali Creek,' Wade had said. 'We'll sit together in the evenings after dinner, on the patio, in the cool and quiet after the day's work, and heat, and tell each other all about ourselves.' That seemed so very long ago, thought Lorna, and it was a relief when eventually the meal was eaten and she could escape. Wade, dressed in tight jeans and a wide-brimmed hat, could be seen a moment or two later, sauntering towards the home paddock where Simon the rouseabout had his horse, a massive chestnut gelding called Gladiator, ready for him to mount. From her bedroom window Lorna broodingly followed the centaur-like figure as, after an effortless swing which took him into the saddle, Wade rode along by the paddock for a while before suddenly cutting across country towards the mob of cattle grazing in the far distance.

What an impressive picture – the man and horse as one, racing across the bush, both in harmony, both thoroughly enjoying the sensation of grace and effortless speed.

With sudden resolution Lorna turned away. She would not continue like this – allowing her mind to dwell on what might have been. Wade was irrevocably lost to her and she must begin the process of regarding him merely as an old acquaintance, someone it had

36

been inordinately pleasant to be with, but who now was unimportant in her life. She went along to her aunt's room and knocked on the door.

'Come in.'

'Auntie, are you feeling better? I haven't wakened you, have I?'

'No, dear, I wasn't sleeping.' She looked at her niece with deep anxiety in her pale blue eyes. 'Lorna . . . oh, my dear child, you've no idea how greatly I regret having brought you here. Has – has Wade told you – anything about himself?'

Lorna put on a bright smile.

'He told me he's engaged to be married.'

Her aunt looked at her in astonishment.

'You don't appear to be in the least upset about it?'

'No, I'm not.' Lorna glanced away. 'It's strange, isn't it, Auntie, how we keep an image in our minds for years, believing the image will never change, that it will still be the same if and when we encounter it again? Having met Wade again after all this time I find I'm not attracted to him any more, not in the least.'

Aunt Bertha stared from where she lay on the bed.

'Are you speaking the truth?' she asked suspiciously after a while, and without hesitation Lorna nodded her head.

'It's just – just gone, Auntie. I like Wade, but that's about all.' Aware of her aunt's keen regard, Lorna turned her face and managed to look her in the eyes.

'What a relief!' exclaimed Aunt Bertha, and gave a heartfelt sigh. 'You have no idea how I've been since learning that Wade is engaged – he mentioned it after you'd left us, and I felt quite sick with guilt, Lorna, believe me, since it was I who had insisted you come out here and see just how Wade was after all this time.

37

You see, I believed, somehow, that he too would have still been in love. I couldn't come down to lunch, couldn't face you just at that time. However, as you're recovered there's no reason for me to worry about my conscience.' She paused a moment, frowning thoughtfully. 'It's a pity, though, for you're both such nice people. I do hope this fiancée of his will make a suitable wife for him.'

'He would hardly have chosen her had he not been sure of that, Auntie.'

'No, I suppose not. Oh, well—' with a shrug as she sat up and patted her hair, '—we're here now, so we might as well enjoy ourselves.'

Lorna looked affectionately at her.

'It was all for me, wasn't it?' she said. 'You're very sweet, Auntie. I'm glad I've got you.'

Her aunt's voice was a trifle gruff as she responded,

'I'm glad I've got you, my dear.' But then she added, 'All the same, I'd be far happier if I knew you were settled, for I shan't be here always. When we get back home you really must look round for a nice husband. I expect you will, now that you've discovered you don't love Wade any more.'

Lorna merely nodded obligingly and turned away to the door.

'I'm going for a walk,' she said, forcing a smile. 'I'll see you at teatime.'

CHAPTER THREE

THE raucous laughter of a kookaburra was the cause of Lorna's awakening with a start the following morning. No one had warned her of these birds and, jumping out of bed, she crossed to the window. She saw nothing at first, but then Dinah appeared with some titbits and the bird swooped down from its perch on the Red River gum tree, its mocking laughter bursting forth again as it did so.

'Well, imagine that!' She found herself responding to his laughter. 'He's as good as any alarm clock.'

The sunrise spread a shower of gold over the wide bushlands and the distant mountain slopes. As far as the eye could see the prospect was one of cattle country where the spinifex, symbol of the Inland, reared its waving plumes of edible oats. It was hard and fearsome country, she thought, her eyes straying to the faraway foothills, now a maze of light and shade as the sun rose higher in the sky. Harsh, weathered country, and yet it possessed a beauty and appeal all its own. Without doubt it seemed more man's country than woman's — the domain of toughened fighters who could sustain the battle against nature's hostility, of slow-spoken bronzed giants like Wade Harcourt whose ancestors, those intrepid pioneers who had been the first to challenge the wild rangelands, had paved the way for the present prosperity enjoyed by the Outback graziers.

Lorna's gaze moved to the colony of stockmen's homes, neat and colourful and set in pretty gardens. There were other 'villages' in various parts of the station, she had learned last evening from the con-

39

versation taking place between Wade and Aunt Bertha, and in consequence, other schools and stores. Wade had two airstrips, one of which was not far from the homestead. From here he flew to the capital when necessary, or to Yarralinga, the nearest town.

'If either of you want to do some shopping, or even merely to look around, I'll willingly take you,' Wade had offered, though still addressing Aunt Bertha rather than her niece. 'I shall be going into town in about three weeks' time.'

On the whole it had not been an unpleasant evening, mused Lorna as she took a shower. True, Wade had talked mainly to her aunt, but she, Lorna, had been quite content to listen. Once or twice Wade had given her a moment's attention, seeming to be drawn to her face now and then, but not once had his features relaxed in a smile for her. And how she had yearned for one of those smiles which she remembered so well, and which she had seen in memory so often during those unhappy years spent with Jack. That smile would bring pleasure, comfort – and even a little thrill of ecstasy on occasions – to brighten her life and lift her briefly from the dull routine of work and thankless endeavour.

Having showered and dressed Lorna made her way to the breakfast-room shown her by Dinah yesterday. Wade was there already, standing, so straight and tall, by the window, looking out to where the mob of Droughtmaster cattle grazed the endless plains. Turning slowly as he heard her enter, Wade allowed his dispassionate eyes to settle on her face for a while.

'Did you sleep well?' he inquired politely at last.

'Yes, thank you, Wade.' Lorna managed a bright smile and glanced around her. She had made only a cursory inspection of the room yesterday, but now she

40

took in the polished hardwood floor, the cedar panelling and the solid Regency sideboard adorned with silver dishes. 'The rooms here are quite delightful,' she exclaimed without thinking. 'Your home is lovely, Wade!'

A small silence followed and she felt her colour rise. It could all have been hers, she felt he was saying, but not in any nostalgic or regretful way, for her quick perceptive gaze could not possibly miss the indifference in his. Suddenly acutely conscious of the fact that he had never wanted her to come here to Bali Creek, Lorna glanced away, aware of the hurtful little lump that had gathered in her throat. She said, still without looking at him,

'I'll go up and see what's happened to Auntie. She should have been down by now. She always gets up early—'

'You aunt rang for Dinah,' Wade cut in quietly. 'She's having her breakfast in bed.'

Lorna frowned.

'That's not like Auntie. She mustn't be well.' Lorna added that she would go up and see her, ending with an awkward, 'If you'll excuse me, Wade?'

'Certainly. But she seemed all right to Dinah.'

'She did?' with relief. 'Then perhaps she's just tired. All the same, I'll run up, just make sure she's not unwell.'

'No, dear,' her aunt answered when Lorna made her anxious inquiry, 'I'm not in the least unwell. But I had a slight headache earlier and rang for Dinah to bring me water so I could take a tablet. She then offered to bring me my breakfast in bed, so I decided to pamper myself. After all, I am on holiday, aren't I?'

'Of course, darling.' Lorna could not prevent herself from glancing at the cut glass water bottle, with its

41

matching unturned tumbler, which she knew had been on the bedside table all the time. 'Are you getting up soon?' she asked curiously.

'Oh, yes. I don't want to spend my time unprofitably. I'm intending to get about and enjoy the scenery and the sun.' A small pause and then, 'You had better go down now, Lorna dear, for I expect Wade won't start his breakfast until you join him.'

Lorna hesitated. The prospect of a meal alone with Wade was far from attractive – after her experience of the lunch yesterday. But she would have to go and join her host, she decided with a faint sigh, and a few minutes later she was sitting opposite to him and, to her surprise, enjoying her breakfast.

'If you would like to ride, Lorna,' he said unexpectedly when the meal was over and they had risen from the table, 'you can have a horse.'

'I'd love to ride, yes. Thank you very much, Wade.'

'I'll tell Simon to find you something— Juno, I think. She's a rather attractively mottled grey mare, and very well behaved.' He looked straight at Lorna, a sudden sternness in his eyes. 'Keep the homestead in sight. That's an order, not advice. You do understand?'

Lorna inclined her head.

'Yes, of course.'

'There's danger for yourself and considerable inconvenience to others in straying too far into the bush tracks. That also goes for walking, of course. If you and your aunt should by any chance decide you wanted to take a long and strenuous hike then let me know and I'll have someone accompany you.'

'Thank you very much, Wade.' She smiled up at him, but as usual no responding smile was forthcoming.

42

'I expect we shall do a good deal of walking. Auntie loves it, and since I went to live with her I've come to enjoy walking too.'

'You didn't do much before then? Your aunt told me you never went out at all – except to go to work and back.'

'That's right.' Lorna was frowning slightly, wondering how much more her aunt had revealed after she, Lorna, had left them together on the verandah after dinner last night.

Wade was looking at her, as if he expected some further comment, but she remained silent and with a polite word of excuse he left the room, saying he would see her and her aunt at lunch time.

Lorna saw him before then, however, for, on going out to Simon to collect her horse, she found him in conversation with the rouseabout.

'I came for the horse,' she said as both men stopped speaking on her approach.

'I'll have her saddled in a jiffy, miss,' said Simon obligingly, and went off to collect Juno from the paddock where she was cropping grass along with several newly-broken brumbies.

'Have I come at an inconvenient time?' asked Lorna half apologetically, her limpid violet eyes lifted to Wade's impassive face.

'Not at all. It doesn't matter when you come. I'd told Simon to expect you.'

She looked him over, her glance taking in the slouch hat, turned down at the sides and up at the front, the checked shirt and belted denims, the dusty leather boots.

'Aren't you riding today?' she had to speak, to terminate the uncomfortable silence that had ensued on the rouseabout's departure for the paddock.

43

'Later. I have other things to attend to at the moment.' He leant against a gate, his long lean body relaxed, his brown fingers tucked into the belt which rested on his hips.

'It must be fascinating work – on the land, I mean?'

'It's interesting,' came the non-committal rejoinder, followed by another silence, and it was a relief when Simon returned and Lorna could mount the horse, watched by the critical eyes of Wade and the curious ones of Simon. Simon was huge, and toughened like old much-polished leather; his gnarled hands on the bridle shone like burnished bronze.

To her surprise the mare bucked a little and Lorna cast Wade a questioning glance, her expression a reminder of his earlier assertion that Juno was well-behaved.

'That's funny,' from Simon who was frowning at the mare's tossing mane.

'She hasn't been ridden for a while,' commented Wade, who also wore a slight frown.

Lorna had not been on a horse for over four years and she must unconsciously have betrayed the tinge of apprehension she felt, because quite suddenly and unexpectedly Wade made up his mind to accompany her on her ride.

'But no—' she began to protest, staring at him, so staggered was she by his offer. 'You have more important things to do.'

'They can wait for an hour. Simon, fetch me Gladiator.'

'Yes, Boss – one minute!'

Less than five minutes after they had started the mare settled down and for a few breathless moments Lorna expected to hear Wade say she could now safely

44

take the ride alone, but with the passing of another five minutes or so she breathed evenly again.

Their ride took them into the bush tracks and eventually the stately Georgian outline of the homestead was lost to view. Wade knew the country like the back of his hand, but to Lorna it was just a maze and involuntarily she shuddered at the thought of finding herself lost in this vast unfriendly wilderness.

'How does our country strike you?' inquired Wade urbanely, casting her a glance as they rode side by side along a dusty gibber track. 'Or is it too soon for you to have gained any definite impression?'

Lorna replied at once.

'It's rather frightening country—'

'Frightening?'

'I think it's the impression of illimitable space and isolation that makes me feel that way. It's inhospitable – the vastness, I mean.'

'So you're not favourably impressed?'

'Oh, but I am! I find a strange – compelling beauty in everything. Already I seem to have become attuned to the – well, bizarre colour that affects parts of the land – like the mountains and the shimmering plains when the sun catches the higher parts. There are so many contrasts even in the immediate region of the homestead – the colours of the trees and flowers and the house itself, being so mellowed with the weathering of the stone, and with the varied creepers growing up its walls.' She was carried away, forgetful of everything except the impressions and sensations she had been receiving from the very moment of stepping on to Australian soil. 'I'm enjoying the complete change, Wade. Even the birds are different.'

'The jacko? You heard him at daybreak?' Wade spoke casually enough, but Lorna gained the unmistakable impression that he had been deeply sensible of her enthusiasm and the warmth of her tones. 'He comes for scraps from Dinah.'

'Yes, I did, and I wondered at first whatever it could be, laughing like that.'

For the first time she saw humour in that austere countenance; it was revealed in the crinkly lines round his eyes as they closed more tightly together and by the faint twitching of his lips, a mannerism, she recalled with poignant intensity, which once had sent her pulses tingling in the most delicious way ... and could have done so now had she not sternly held herself in check.

'His laughter's usually infectious.' The merest pause and then, 'Did he make you laugh, Lorna?'

'Yes, indeed!' She shone at him, because suddenly she was inordinately happy, owing to the slight softening in his manner with her, and because she felt that he might not now be regarding her as an unwelcome guest, but as an old friend whom he would never quite forget.

'I think we'll take a little rest,' Wade suggested half an hour later as they reached the cut-off lake around which grew in profusion the sturdy old patriarch of the eucalypt family, the Red River gum.

'Is this what is called a billabong?' Lorna wanted to know when, the horses tethered, they were sitting on the banks of the cut-off.

'That's right.' Wade leant back against a tree and stretched his long legs out in front of him. 'Do you know anything about physical geography?' he then asked, and she shook her head. 'Oh, well, never mind.'

'Please go on,' she urged, trying not to reveal how she felt — eager and happy, and grateful for a few

46

memories which she might take home with her when the time arrived for her to say good-bye to Wade. 'You were going to explain about the billabong?'

Wade turned his head, gazing at her profile. Conscious of his stare, she also turned her head, a smile quivering. Wade's lids came down; he said after a strange little silence,

'It's difficult to explain to those who have no knowledge at all, but, in the simplest way, a billabong is formed when a river cuts off a meander. This usually happens in flood time, when the volume and rush of water surging along the river bed has no time, as it were, to go running round the curve. So it takes a short cut and runs across it—' As he spoke Wade was mechanically making a diagram with his finger, on the ground between him and Lorna. 'A lake is left because the river deposits silt which stops up the ends. You call this an oxbow lake or a cut-off; we call it a billabong. It is in fact a loop of river and can be small or quite large, depending on the original size of the meander.'

'So a billabong is always close to a river?' She was gazing away towards the bed of Bali Creek, dry now, until the Wet which would begin in December, when the rains came.

'In the main, yes. There are exceptions, but these have to do with changes in the courses of a river and are rather technical. They wouldn't interest you, anyway.'

Lorna was staring into the waters of the billabong.

'It looks as if it's always been here,' she murmured, trying to imagine what the original course of the river was like before the cut-off occurred.

'It's been here for many hundreds of years,' Wade told her. 'You can tell that by its distance from the river. Much material has been deposited between the

47

two, as you can see.' He was looking at his wrist watch as he spoke, and Lorna experienced a little access of dejection as she realized it was time they were getting back to the homestead.

But to her surprise Wade seemed in no particular hurry to move. On the contrary, he actually made himself more comfortable against the supporting trunk of the tree.

'Do you take time off from your work?' asked Lorna, voicing what was in her thoughts.

'Sometimes – not very often.'

She said, not in any way because she wanted to, but because she was driven by some strange urge to talk about the girl he was going to marry,

'Olga ... you go and stay with her parents?'

'On occasions, and they come to me at times.'

'I expect,' she said, trying to sound off-hand about it, 'that when you're married you'll not work quite so hard?'

'I shall take more time off, I suppose.' He sounded, she thought, as if he were not quite sure. 'A wife has a right to expect to see her husband around now and then.'

Now and then. ... There was something cool and dispassionate about the way he said that, decided Lorna, and began to wonder what sort of a girl Olga was. Perhaps she also was a little dispassionate, in which case the two would be eminently suited.

'You've changed—' The words came out unbidden and Lorna would have done anything to take them back.

'Changed?' Wade turned to look at her. 'In what way have I changed?' He was plainly curious to know what her reply would be, and as there was no chance of evasion Lorna had no option than to tell the truth.

'You're . . . harder, Wade, and a little cynical, I think.'

'Harder.' He thought about this, his grey eyes narrowed, his brows knitted together. 'Yes, I expect one does harden with the passing of time. And I'm cynical too – or am I? You were not quite sure?"

'You're different, very different,' she said, and looked down at her slender hands, clasped together tightly.

'I'm older,' he said, and suddenly there was a repelling quality about him that struck Lorna forcibly. They were moving towards dangerous ground, she realized, ground that should be avoided if past bitternesses he had experienced at her hands were not to be raked up. No unpleasant memory of friction between Wade and herself must mar this visit to his country, Lorna decided, and tactfully changed the subject.

'Tell me about your work, Wade. You have such a fantastically large place here; I'd no idea that it was of such vast dimensions. It must be an enormous responsibility, running the estate. Do you have lots of people helping you with the paper work?'

If Wade guessed why she had swung the conversation he made no betrayal of it, and his rich Australian drawl was pleasant enough as he replied,

'One man helps me in that respect: Robert Mowbray. You'll be meeting him this evening. He lives at one of the bungalows but dines with me twice a week, when we usually discuss business, but not when I have guests, of course.'

'Is he a bachelor?'

Wade nodded.

'He came this way in his car one day last year when he was on vacation from his office in Brisbane. The city

49

life was beginning to pall, he said, and I asked him what he did. When he told me I saw at once that he could be useful to me and I offered him a job. He went off back to Brisbane to give in – and work – his notice. He then packed his belongings and was back here within a month. He's taken a lot of work off my hands, making life much easier than it used to be when I did all the office work myself.' Wade paused for a moment.

'What else do you want to know about the station? If you're going to be here for any length of time you'll find it all out for yourself.'

'I don't know how long we're staying, Wade. As I said, we mustn't stay so long that we become a nuisance.'

He seemed to consider this.

'You must stay as long as you like, Lorna. I can't see either you or your aunt becoming a nuisance.'

She gave him a tremulous smile.

'Thank you, Wade. It's kind of you to say that.'

'Kind?' He raised an eyebrow quizzically. It was another mannerism she had once come to know so well and despite her resolution to forget his attractions, now she knew for sure that he was not for her, she did experience a tiny thrill of pleasure, and even excitement, as she stared into his face. 'I seem to remember your telling me I was hard.'

'Hard people can be kind on occasions,' she rejoined evasively, and the trace of a smile touched his lips, and hovered there a while.

'I'm afraid,' he decided presently, 'that we must be making tracks for home. I hope you've enjoyed your first ride on Juno?'

'Very much,' she answered softly, and wondered what he would think were he to know just what the

50

ride had meant to her. He never would know, and the idea hurt so abominably that she wished she were alone and could cry.

Olga and her parents, Mr. and Mrs. Norville, arrived the day before Wade's other guests, and judging by the way they immediately made themselves at home, it was easy to see they were used to visiting the man who was soon to become one of the family. On being introduced to Olga, Lorna received something of a shock, for the girl was totally different in appearance from anything Lorna had expected. True, she had known Wade's fiancée was dark, but she had not expected anyone from the Outback to be so flawlessly beautiful or so elegantly turned out. Her lovely hair, shining blue-black against a peaches-and-cream skin, was long and straight, and springy with health. Olga knew this latter was an asset, for she would repeatedly toss her head so that the natural – and most attractive – sway of the hair would bring attention to herself.

If Lorna received a shock it would appear that Olga received an even greater one as, extending a hand, she instantly gave a start on looking into Lorna's face. The dark eyes then narrowed in the most peculiar way before being lifted to those of Wade, who apparently saw nothing amiss, for he merely gave his fiancée a smile.

'How do you do, Miss Norville.' Lorna also smiled at the girl, but in response there was only a widening of those dark eyes to take in the clear picture of Lorna, with her pale gold hair and delicately-moulded features. When several seconds passed and no smile appeared Lorna's lips straightened out. She felt she had been snubbed. The handshake, too, was lacking in warmth. But it was not only a snub which Lorna experienced; there was something profoundly tense in the atmosphere.

'Wade, darling,' purred Olga, lifting her face as he stood above her, 'you said something over the air about Mrs. Trent's being an old friend. . . . Or have I made a mistake?'

Sharply both Wade and Lorna looked at her, for there was so strange an inflection in her voice. Wade seemed inwardly to frown, but there was nothing indicative of this in his tone when he spoke.

'No, Olga, you're not mistaken. Lorna and I met a few years ago when I was on a visit to England to see relatives – you must recall my going?' he added, and slowly his fiancée nodded.

'Was Mrs. Trent married at that time?' The question was totally irrelevant and now a frown actually appeared on Wade's brow.

'No, as a matter of fact, she wasn't,' and he moved with an abruptness that was very noticeable indeed. Olga's narrowed gaze followed his tall figure as he went towards the place where the drinks were arrayed, on a beautiful oak sideboard, Georgian and solid.

'Shall we sit here?' Lorna indicated a window-seat, wide and cretonne-covered.

Olga's glance was one of deep animosity and Lorna's pulse quickened. What was the matter with the girl?

'You appear already to have made yourself at home – very much so.' But then she shrugged her shoulders and added, 'We might as well sit here. One place is as good as another.'

Lorna's glance was extremely puzzled as she looked sideways at the girl who was engaged to Wade. The open animosity, that start of surprise which had been the forerunner of this animosity. . . . What did it all mean? The question put to Wade about Lorna's being married when first he knew her. . . . It would almost seem that Olga knew of that old love affair between Lorna and Wade . . . but as she knew for sure that no mention of it would have been made by him to his fiancée Lorna instantly dismissed the idea, little knowing just how soon it was to come up again.

Her eyes remained on Olga's set profile. Surely she could adopt a friendly manner, which was normal with guests, even if she did happen to take a dislike to someone. Lorna was sure that Olga had taken an instant dislike to her, but for what reason she could not for the life of her make out.

'Your home is about a hundred miles away, Wade tells me.' Lorna decided to make an attempt at friendly conversation, foreseeing awkwardness and discomfort both for herself and Olga if the girl could not be coaxed into a more amicable mood.

'Over a hundred.' A pause, then a dazzling smile as Wade came across with their drinks. He was in a cream-coloured tropical suit, perfectly cut so that it seemed to be part of his long lean body. How distinguished he looked, thought Lorna, a catch in her heart despite her determination that she would exercise a stern control over her emotions, never losing sight for one single moment of the fact that he was not for her. Not for her. . . . Lorna twisted her fair head and glanced at her companion. Olga's eyes were shining as they looked up into those of her fiancé, her long tapering fingers deliberately touched his as she took the glass from him. This girl was his choice, this immaculate girl who, thought Lorna, would do very well in some exclusive Paris fashion house, modelling creations fit for a queen.

'Thank you, Wade,' gushed Olga, fluttering her long curling lashes in the most alluring way. Lorna

53

thought, 'How very strange that he should have chosen someone the exact opposite to me, not only in colouring and the way she dresses, but also in the way she is – in herself. She's so self-assured and so cold, somehow. . . .' But then, Lorna told herself, Wade was now rather cold, and as she had told him, he was hard. The man she had known was gone, the smiling eager lover whose only hardness was in his body, whose only severity was when on occasions he felt it necessary to portray a little mastery. This until the day of awful parting, when she had known a fury she would never have believed he possessed. That fury had died through the years and on meeting her again he was the urbane host, the well-bred gentleman who had extended politeness to her even though it had been his wish that she stay away from Bali Creek.

'Your drink, Lorna. You seem to be daydreaming.' She glanced at him as he spoke and took the glass from his hand.

'Thank you,' she murmured, and immediately looked away, for his eyes had strayed back to those of his fiancée and for a moment or two he and Olga made casual conversation.

'Wade mentioned that you're a widow,' said Olga on his moving away to join the other three who were chatting together by the fireplace. 'You're very young to be widowed.' Lorna said nothing and after a moment Olga added, 'Just why did your aunt decide to pay this visit to Wade?'

'My aunt won some money, and as she's always wanted to travel she immediately thought of Wade—'

'I wonder why?' rudely interrupted Olga, sending a glance in the old lady's direction. 'Why here, I mean?'

54

Lorna shrugged, at a loss for the moment. She could hardly come out with the truth: that her aunt had hoped for a reconciliation between Wade and her niece – the girl he had once chosen for his wife.

'Not for any particular reason,' she replied at last. 'Auntie thought she would like to visit Australia, and as Wade was the only person she knew here she naturally wrote asking if we could come for a visit.'

A small silence followed, a strange and chill sort of hush which made Lorna wish she could find an excuse for getting up and leaving this girl to whatever thoughts were so intensely occupying her mind.

'Your aunt doesn't seem like the travelling kind,' musingly from Olga at length. 'How odd that she should want to come here, to the Outback.' The dark eyes reflected an ill-humour that was as sudden as it was incomprehensible. 'This is scarcely the place to which one would come if it were one's intention to see something of our country. The towns, and the reef islands and places like the Top End with its wild life and the safaris available to tourists; these are the obvious attractions one would look for. The Outback has nothing at all to offer.'

Lorna felt her mouth tighten. What had it got to do with Olga, the choice her aunt had made?

'I wouldn't agree that the Outback has nothing,' she argued in cool and indignant tones. 'It has peace and space and in fact is a totally different world from what we know back home. Here one is a world away from the maelstrom of rush and bustle, from traffic and its horried fumes, from factories and all the smoke and smells which industry of that kind invariably creates.'

'You are enthusiastic, aren't you?' with distinct sarcasm and a faintly contemptuous curl of Olga's car-

55

mine lips. 'All the same, if you're honest you'll agree with me that we here have comparatively little to offer the tourist?'

'We aren't really tourists,' Lorna began, then stopped abruptly on noting the sudden narrowing of the girl's eyes.

'You're not . . .? This is a private visit, then?'

How subtle the girl was; how cleverly she seemed to be pulling Lorna into some sort of a net.

'It's merely a friendly visit to Wade's home,' she explained, trying not to reveal her impatience at Olga's attitude. 'Auntie chose the Outback and I obviously adhered to her choice. After all, it was her money that brought us out here.'

Dark the glance which Lorna received in response to this admission, dark with a mingling of contempt and hauteur. Plainly the girl considered herself far superior to Wade's visitors from England.

'Your aunt was indeed fortunate in having her win – it was a win you mentioned, wasn't it?' Lorna nodded and she continued, 'Had she not been so fortunate then you couldn't have taken the trip?'

'Her winnings paid for it,' replied Lorna quietly, trying to catch her aunt's eye and convey to her that she was required to come over and rescue her niece. But Aunt Bertha was chatting happily with her host and the Norvilles, neither of whom appeared to possess the arrogance and supercilious manner inherent in their daughter.

'As I was saying,' pursued Olga after sipping her drink in silence for a few moments, 'the Outback has nothing to offer to tourists, and I said that if you're honest you'll readily agree with me.'

A frown knit Lorna's wide brow. What was Olga working for? She seemed determined to get Lorna to

56

admit that the Outback had nothing to offer, but why? It were simpler to give her what she wanted, thought Lorna with a little inner shrug of resignation.

'You said it had comparatively little,' she corrected, then added before Olga could speak, 'You're right, I suppose. The rest of the country *has* much more to offer the tourists.'

'In fact,' suddenly purred the girl, 'you now do admit that the Outback's monotonous country with no facilities for entertainment? In effect, it's rather dull?'

Lorna's frown deepened. Innocently she said,

'I suppose, in comparison to the entertainments one finds in the towns and the seaside resorts, and on the islands you have mentioned, the Outback would appear dull and uninteresting to some people.'

The girl nodded her head in a satisfied kind of way. What a strange person, thought Lorna. Well, if the admission satisfied her and put a stop to the stupid persistence, then so much to the good. It wasn't until dinner was over and Wade and his guests were seated on the verandah with their coffee and liquers that enlightenment came to Lorna, and when it did it quite literally staggered her, not only by the way in which her innocently-spoken words were twisted almost out of recognition, but also by the fact of Olga's wishing to convey to Wade something that was so far removed from the truth.

'Mrs. Trent and I were having an interesting little chat before dinner, as you would no doubt have noticed?' Olga began by way of introduction to what was to follow.

'I did see that you were conversing,' agreed Wade with a glance at Lorna. 'I expect two young women of similar age had a good deal to talk about.'

57

'Indeed yes,' with charming enthusiasm from Olga, who was now a totally different person from the superior and condescending girl who had earlier shared the window-seat with Lorna and adopted so unfriendly an attitude towards her. 'We were, quite naturally, talking of Mrs. Trent's visit, and she was saying that the Outback's dreadfully dull and uninteresting. She thinks it's monotonous country with no facilities for entertainment, and says she wished she and her aunt had based themselves in a town, from where they could have visited some of the coral islands, and the nature reserves. I expect she would have liked to see the corroborees that are arranged for the tourists, and gone on one or two safaris.'

Lorna just gasped inwardly at this blatant yet effective manipulation of the words which Olga herself had deliberately put into Lorna's mouth. Wade had stiffened visibly, and his grey eyes had narrowed suddenly. Under his almost accusing stare Lorna lowered her eyes, a sickening sensation having settled in her stomach. What should she do? A denial would of a surety result in an argument, as it was transparently plain that Olga had said what she had in order to alienate Wade in his attitude towards Lorna, and, therefore, it was reasonable to assume she would argue with Lorna should she deny having said that the Outback was dull and uninteresting. She *had* said the words, so she could scarcely deny this. The qualification she had made would, if repeated, sound like an excuse, voiced simply because Wade was here – Wade, her host whose hospitality she was enjoying. What must he be thinking of her? Lorna wondered, unutterable despair taking possession of her. Another factor in the situation was that, should Lorna decide to try and rectify the impression Wade now had, it would seem she was making out his fiancée to be a liar, which was scarcely the thing to do. Besides, there was nothing to be gained by such an action, since obviously Wade would accept Olga's word in preference to hers.

'So already you're bored?' No forgetting he was her host, but although the slow Australian drawl was polite it was unmistakably edged with ice. 'That was not the impression you gave me earlier, when we were out riding.'

'Out riding?' Olga's dark eyes flashed to Lorna, whose own eyes remained downcast, for they were far too bright, and her lips were beginning to quiver uncontrollably, reflecting the utter misery within her. 'You actually went out riding, Wade? But you're always too busy when *I* ask you to come riding.' Her voice had reached a higher pitch and, carried as it was to the others, chatting round their table a little distance along the verandah, they all glanced up, their attitudes questioning.

Wade was frowning at his fiancée.

'I can't remember,' he said after a rather cool hesitation. 'In any case, what does it matter?'

Olga went a trifle red, realizing that her protest was childish and irrelevant to the subject under discussion.

'I'm not bored,' said Lorna in answer to Wade's earlier question. 'Far from it.' But she knew that her words had made no impression on him. His glance was cold, indifferent, and as the evening progressed his avoidance of drawing her into the conversation became very marked indeed. Lorna saw her aunt's eyes on her several times, and there was the most odd expression in their depths. There was an element of preocccupation about her too, and she would withdraw from the conversation voluntarily, and lean back in her chair, her

59

pale eyes moving from Wade to Olga and then to her niece.

Olga scintillated like a star. She knew all the tricks, decided Lorna — the gestures with her hands which brought to notice their smooth whiteness and long painted nails, the widening of her eyes, the toss of that proud head which caused her beautiful hair to sway so enchantingly. Often Wade's attention was fixed upon it and Lorna would wonder if his hands were itching to run through it or. . . .

With a catch of pain that was almost physical Lorna recalled how he would gather her hair into one of his hands, as he held her close, and gently tug at it, forcing her head back so that he could take possession of her lips. It was a masterful gesture, a manifestation of the dominance he intended exerting over her.

What a bitter blow to his pride when she gave him up . . . this in addition to the hurt she had inflicted on his heart, for he had loved her dearly, and she would remember to her dying day that look of sheer anguish when for one brief lull in his fury he had begged her to reconsider before ruining both their lives. They belonged together, he had declared fiercely, they were made for each other. . . .

And now he had chosen another girl, a cold girl and, Lorna felt certain, a mercenary one. Her brother, Brock, who had been mentioned several times during the dinner-table conversation, would inherit the ranch of his father; Olga would be mistress of an even larger estate, that of Bali Creek.

CHAPTER FOUR

LORNA and Brock met a fortnight after she and her aunt had come to Wade's home. Brock had happened to be on hand when the car driven by the two students from the agricultural college broke down. Having tried to get it going without success, Brock had taken the students home to Blue River Downs, where they stayed the night. The following morning he drove them over to Bali Creek, promising to get someone to repair their car and drive it out to them.

'We're terribly grateful,' said Richard, a good-looking young man of twenty-one whose eyes flickered with admiration on sighting Lorna, who was strolling towards the terrace where the four men stood. Wade introduced her, oblivious of Richard's interest but not, apparently, of Brock's. For his grey eyes narrowed a little on his noticing just how long Olga's brother held Lorna's hand in his.

'You didn't tell us she was so devastatingly pretty!' he exclaimed in laughing tones. 'And she can blush, too! How enchantingly naïve. Lorna, we must get to know one another better!'

'You'll soon discover,' commented Wade in that cool slow drawl of his, 'that Brock is the Outback's greatest flirt.'

Another laugh from Brock. He released Lorna's hand but kept his admiring gaze fixed upon her face.

'I shouldn't have thought there were many girls with whom to flirt,' said Lorna and, catching Wade's eye, she reddened a little, aware that he was recalling Olga's assertion that she, Lorna, had described the

61

Outback as dull and uninteresting.

'There are a fair number,' returned Brock. 'You'll be meeting some of them when we have our woodshed dance next week.'

'Next week?' Wade glanced questioningly at him. 'Olga didn't mention any shed dance.'

'Mother only made her mind up this morning. You know what she is: tardy for weeks, then once she's made up her mind it has to be done right away. I've invited Richard and David here, and now I've passed the news on to you. We'll expect you a week today, Wade – and don't forget to bring Lorna and her aunt.'

'Thanks, Brock. You're not going yet?'

'I'd like to get back before dark.'

Wade looked at the powerful overlanding car, standing on the forecourt of the house.

'It won't take you more than a couple of hours, despite the state of the roads around these parts. Once off the tracks you'll do ninety miles an hour.'

'Yes, you're right,' agreed Brock, and accepted Wade's offer to stay for a snack.

'Dinah's here,' said Wade to the two students. 'She'll show you your rooms. I've had small desks put up there, just in case you prefer to do your writing in complete privacy.'

'That's very kind of you, sir.' David turned to follow the lubra, but Richard seemed reluctant to go. His appreciative gaze was on Lorna's face again and Wade said, with a distinct edge of sarcasm in his tone,

'Was there something you required, young man?'

Richard coloured, as well he might, and without further hesitation turned and followed in the wake of the lubra and his friend.

'Glad you put that young cub in his place,' frowned

62

Brock immediately he was out of earshot. 'Too darned interested in Lorna for my liking.'

Wade looked at him, and then transferred his attention to Lorna. She was pink-cheeked with embarrassment, murmuring, just because she had to say something,

'You're quite wrong, Mr. Norville. He's no more than a boy.'

'Brock's the name. I've never been called Mr. Norville for years.'

Lorna had to laugh; and it helped dispel her discomfiture.

'I don't know if I should call you Brock on so short an acquaintance.' How different he was from his sister, she thought. It seemed quite extraordinary that he could be so spontaneously friendly while she was so openly hostile.

'She's nice, isn't she?' Brock asked the question of Wade, who frowned as if the man's persistence annoyed him. Or perhaps he was bored by it, mused Lorna as she watched him stifle a yawn.

'Perhaps you'd like to have a wash and brush up before your snack. You know the room you always have, so there's no need for me to call Dinah.'

'No, of course not. See you later,' he added buoyantly, and went off to his room.

Lorna and Wade were left alone; there had existed a degree of coolness on his part ever since those malicious words were spoken by his fiancée. But he was ever the polite host, and if she should not appear to have an appetite, or she should look tired after a long tramp taken in company with her aunt, Wade would anxiously question her, or proffer advice.

'You shouldn't ride in the heat of the afternoon,' he had sternly admonished on one occasion. And on

63

another he had actually sent her up to bed immediately after dinner.

'You ought not to have tramped so far,' he said when she protested that it was far too early to go to bed. 'I'll see Seth doesn't keep you out so long again. It's a wonder he himself didn't get tired and decide to turn back.'

After watching his expression for some time after he had finished speaking Aunt Bertha said,

'Blame me, Wade. Seth did want to return sooner, but I was in a fighting fit mood and I thought to myself: what's the good of returning, and just sitting around until dinner time, when I can walk another four or five miles in the lovely fresh air?'

Faintly Wade smiled. He liked Aunt Bertha, no mistake about that.

'You could have taken a siesta rather than sit around,' he pointed out. 'It's quite usual for visitors to do so. As for the fresh air you mention – we do have exactly the same in our own garden, plus comfortable deck chairs and even a hammock.' Transferring his gaze, he said, 'Up to bed, Lorna – and don't read.'

She had risen then, flushing under the order she had received. And she had made no further attempt to argue, as already she had learned that when the Boss of Bali Creek gave an order it was expected instantly to be obeyed.

She and Wade were now on the terrace, he looking down at her from his superior height, she forcing a smile to her lips and willing him to melt, to be a little more affable with her, as he was during that pleasant ride in the bush. Were it not for Olga's vindictiveness he might yet again have ridden with her, Lorna thought. But he hadn't ridden with her and she was once again feeling as if she were the unwelcome guest.

64

'You appear to have made an impression on Brock,' he commented at last, and Lorna gave a small impatient shrug.

'As you said, he's a flirt. One can tell his kind immediately.'

'So you're not one of those who respond to flattery?'

Lorna looked away. She *had* responded to flattery ... his flattery, and she knew for sure that indifferent as he was with her, he was now recalling things past ... intimate things. ...

'I don't respond to flattery from a man like Brock,' she murmured, glancing up at him again, 'because it lacks sincerity.'

A strange silence followed, as the two stood there, in the warm intimacy of the garden where tall palms stood sentinel over carpet-smooth lawns, lawns bordered by hibiscus and poinsettias and dainty oleanders. The lovely temple tree, or frangipani as it was as commonly known, lavished the softly-moving air with a fragrance as enticing as any expensive perfume. The plain shimmered in the heat; in the far distance could faintly be discerned a raw-boned youth swinging lightly into the saddle and setting his horse trotting across the dusty plain towards a line of low hills where cattle grazed under the watchful eyes of the Aboriginal stockriders.

'You'll have difficulty in keeping Brock at a distance, once he's made up his mind to flirt with you.' Wade's soft drawl intruded into the silence. Lorna looked up into inscrutable eyes, unaware of the pretty picture she made – a golden silhouette against the backcloth of the mellowed homestead building whose stately outline was itself enhanced by a frame of ancient trees whose foliage cast shadows to soften the walls and porch and wide, vine-draped verandahs.

'I shall know how to deal with him,' was Lorna's confident rejoinder. 'I'm neither so young, nor so foolish, as to have my head turned by anything he might say to me.'

It was a strange sort of conversation, she mused, her mind inevitably taking another back-switch so that memory surged in. So jealous Wade had been, she recalled. He could not bear her to talk about Jack, to whom she had been engaged for almost three years. Yet now he could without one small degree of emotion discuss the possibility of Brock's flirting with her. 'Our love might never have been,' she whispered to herself, and closed her eyes tightly, because of the insistent tears and the pain in her heart and the regret for all that was lost, for ever. Wade belonged to another girl – a girl who soon would have the right to call him husband, who would be mistress of this lovely Georgian homestead with its elegant high-ceilinged rooms and panelling and its superb setting of lawns and trees and exotic flowers.

'What are you thinking about?' The suddenness of the question and the tone of its delivery caused Lorna to give a visible start. 'Whatever it is it's . . . painful.'

She coloured in the most attractive kind of way.

'It wasn't anything really important, Wade,' she replied evasively. And she said softly, 'Memories. . . .' which she had not meant to say at all and which she soon regretted because she was immediately misunderstood.

'Your husband?' No emotion, no bitterness or regret. As far as Wade was concerned the past was dead, and his question was voiced merely because it was the only one that came to his mind, the only one which could be causing her such painful memories – or so he believed,

66

thought Lorna, reading him so easily. Her answer was destined never to be given, for at that moment Aunt Bertha appeared from the house and they both turned to see her smiling to herself – a rather satisfied smile which could also be described as faintly enigmatic.

'There you are! How happy a picture you make. Wade, I do adore your country! Do you think I might be able to buy a small farm somewhere around – with the money I have?'

The situation was instantly eased, as both Wade and Lorna had to laugh.

'As I have no idea how much money you have, Mrs. Gerrard, I am not in a position to say. What I can say is that we do not have small farms. This terrain is unsuitable for intensive farming as you know it in your country. You might be able to purchase a cattle station, if someone had one for sale—'

'Impertinent young man! I haven't the money nor the inclination to buy a station! What else could I buy? You don't seem to have any house agents around here.'

'Auntie, don't be so idiotic! You haven't the least intention of settling in Australia. Why, you'd be homesick within a month!'

'A month? How long have we been here now?'

'Only two weeks.'

'Two weeks, and I've enjoyed every single moment of it. As I've just said, Wade, I adore your country!'

'It's nice to hear you say that, Mrs. Gerrard.' His eyes flickered to Lorna. 'Your niece isn't quite so enthusiastic, though. She finds it dull and uninteresting here, in the Outback.'

The old lady frowned, and looked interrogatingly at her niece.

'I don't understand? You've told Wade that – and

67

you a guest in his house? You told me you loved it here, becoming all poetical about the silence and peace, and you were absolutely in raptures over the sunrises and sunsets and the colours of the landscape at these times.' She shook her head vigorously. 'I don't believe you said that to Wade.'

He looked at her, his grey eyes narrowing in puzzlement.

'Lorna told you she likes this part of the world?'

'That's what I said.' Aunt Bertha frowned in silence for a space and then, 'Lorna can't have said she doesn't like it here, simply because that wouldn't be true.'

'She didn't, Mrs. Gerrard. But she told my fiancée she found it dull and uninteresting – er – monotonous country, I believe you said, Lorna?' She could find no answer for the moment and Wade added, 'You appear to have given your aunt a totally different impression.'

'It was due to a misunderstanding,' began Lorna, wondering how to handle this without putting Wade's fiancée in a bad light which in consequence would affect Wade himself, causing him to be embarrassed by the knowledge that Olga had deliberately twisted Lorna's words – and for no apparent reason.

'A misunderstanding?' Wade desired a fuller explanation; Lorna saw this at once and tactfully tried to withdraw, putting an end to the inquiry.

'It isn't important, Wade. Miss Norville misinterpreted my words, that's all.' She gave him a forced smile. 'As I said, it isn't important.' She turned to her aunt. 'We're invited to a shed dance at the Norvilles'. Isn't it exciting?'

Ignoring this side-stepping of the issue, her aunt asked,

'In what way did Miss Norville misinterpret your

68

words, Lorna?' Before her niece could reply Aunt Bertha had turned to Wade. 'I hope you don't mind my insistence? I do dislike mysteries. Lorna dear, explain, please.'

But Lorna shook her head, quite unable to find any reason why her aunt should refuse to let the matter drop.

'I too dislike mysteries,' said Wade in firm decisive tones. 'You told me you liked it here and, as with your aunt, you became quite poetical about it. Yet you told Olga a very different story. Can I know why?'

Impatiently she gestured with her hands.

'Can't we let this drop?' she begged, frowning at them in turn. 'I've just said it isn't important.'

'The mystery deepens,' observed Wade softly. 'Lorna, I'll have an explanation from you, if you please.'

She shrugged then, resignedly. Wade would force an answer from her, she was certain of that, and so she related exactly what had occurred, trying as best she could to shield Olga, but she saw at once, by the tightening of Wade's mouth, that he was angry.

'So you didn't say it was dull and uninteresting, and that you'd rather have stayed in a town so that you could have gone places?' It was her aunt who spoke, before Wade had time to do so, and the old lady's voice was fringed with anger. 'In other words, Miss Norville made it all up?'

'Auntie!' exclaimed Lorna involuntarily, horrified by her outspokenness and lack of consideration for Wade's feelings.

'I think,' put in Wade tersely, 'that we can now allow the matter to drop. If you'll excuse me, I have some work to do,' and without another word he was gone.

69

'Auntie ... you were awful!' Lorna chided, cross with her aunt for the very first time. 'You seemed to forget that Miss Norville is his fiancée. It must have been upsetting enough for him to learn that she'd lied, without your rubbing it in, as it were.'

'I intended rubbing it in! I disliked that girl on sight; she's not good enough for a fine man like Wade—'

'He obviously considers she is, and that's all that matters.'

'Then he's a fool – or blind. I can't make it out at all.'

'Make what out?'

'His taking to her in the first place. Anyone can see what she is – with her affected mannerisms and supercilious air! And just now, when it struck me she had lied in order to create a coolness between you and Wade – and he *has* been cool with you since that night. Don't think I haven't noticed it – I insisted on bringing her perfidy out into the open. Why should she get away with it at your expense?'

'It didn't matter, Auntie.' Lorna gave a sigh; she was heartily tired of the whole wretched business, hurt because Wade was hurt. He had gone away to lick his wounds, she surmised, knowing just how disillusioned she herself would be in finding her loved one out in unnecessary deceit. 'I'd rather have left it as it was.'

'You would? Why?'

'Because I don't want Wade to be hurt, of course.'

'And yet you don't love him ... or so you said?'

'I don't love him—' Lorna looked down at her hands, avoiding her aunt's intent scrutiny. 'But that doesn't mean I want him to be hurt and embarrassed. In my opinion it would have been far better to have left him in ignorance.'

70

'What puzzles me,' said Aunt Bertha with a thoughtful expression, 'is why the girl should go to those lengths. There was obviously a reason, but what reason?'

'I must admit it puzzled me too. It seemed so lacking in purpose or sense. What good can it do Olga if Wade is made to believe that I don't like it here?'

Aunt Bertha's mouth was pursed; there was an odd expression in her pale blue eyes.

'I don't know. . . .' she murmured thoughtfully. 'I don't know. . . .'

If Wade had been angry with Olga because of her deliberate lies he had forgotten it by the time he saw her again, which was at the shed dance given by her parents. Wade drove his guests the hundred miles or so in the big homestead car which he parked alongside a number of others outside the huge building in which the dance was held. Olga was there, glowing and smiling and fluttering her eyelashes with the subtlety of the expert. But when her eyes lighted on Lorna the smile faded; she acknowledged her with a slight inclination of her head and turned immediately to the two students, whom Wade had already introduced to her. Aunt Bertha noted the slight and her eyes glittered with anger.

'What a detestable creature!' she exclaimed a long while later when she and Lorna were eating barbecued chicken under the trees some small distance from the shed. 'Wade must be out of his mind!'

'He knows what he's doing, Auntie,' returned Lorna in tones meant to be light. But she herself felt unable to understand Wade's choice. Of course, Olga was clever enough to keep her less attractive side from her fiancé, and as he did not see her very much at all it was quite

71

conceivable that he was in total ignorance of her true character.

'Men are so unfathomable.' Aunt Bertha was in one of her thoughtful moods and her food was now going cold on her plate. 'One never knows what they're about.'

Frowning in bewilderment, Lorna said,

'What do you mean, Auntie?'

'Haven't you noticed that Olga Norville's the exact opposite of what you are?'

'In colouring, you mean? Of course I have.'

'His wife will never remind him of the girl he once loved,' murmured Aunt Bertha, still thoughtful. Her eyes had wandered absently. Wade and Olga were laughing by the long table on which the cold sweets were laid out. Olga's hand was resting on his arm, her cheek pressed to his shoulder. Following the direction of her gaze Lorna knew a sensation of deep pain, and her eyes filled up. If only she could go home, she thought. But her aunt seemed quite settled and as yet there had been no mention of leaving Bali Creek. 'Ah, here's Brock!' exclaimed Aunt Bertha, diverted from her interest in Wade and his glamorous fiancée. 'Sit down, dear boy. Move up, Lorna, and let him come between us.'

'Enjoying yourself?' he asked, glancing at Lorna with undisguised admiration. 'Might I take this opportunity of commenting on your delightful dress?'

'Yes to both questions,' she laughed, recalling for no special reason that rather satisfied smile that had hovered on her aunt's lips the day Brock had driven the two students over to Bali Creek. Lorna had later made some casual remark about Olga's brother having come and had received the reply,

'Yes; I've been chatting with him. He was on his

way to a bedroom when I came from mine. Such a charming young man!' And to Lorna's puzzlement and surprise the satisfied smile had reappeared. Knowing her so well Lorna would in ordinary circumstances have suspected her aunt of 'being up to something', but, as they were here at Bali Creek, taking a holiday, there really wasn't anything she could be up to.

'Your dress is quite the prettiest here tonight,' Brock was saying gallantly. 'And, Lorna, your hair is just about the loveliest I've ever seen.'

His flattery merely had the effect of bringing a laugh from Lorna, a laugh which rang out rather more loudly than she intended, and to her embarrassment Wade and his partner turned their eyes in her direction. Lorna lowered her head ... but not before she had surprised the expression on her aunt's face.

The old lady *was* up to something!

'Why are you looking so satisfied with yourself, Auntie?' Lorna could not help putting the question, for her curiosity could not be contained.

'Satisfied, my dear?' in rather startled tones from her aunt. 'I don't think I understand you?'

Lorna hesitated. It seemed absurd to pursue the matter, but she did say,

'You were looking very gratified about something just then.' When she was looking at Wade, Lorna suddenly realized. Now why should Aunt Bertha look gratified simply because Wade's attention had been arrested by Lorna's laughter?

'It was your imagination, my dear,' stated Aunt Bertha firmly, and Lorna merely gave a small sigh and allowed the matter to rest there. In any case, Brock was speaking again, telling her not to laugh at his compliments, because they were absolutely sincere.

'Now, Brock,' she admonished, 'you know very well

73

you're the Outback's greatest flirt!'

'Wade's accusation,' he scoffed in disgust, his handsome bronzed face pulled into a scowl. 'He's only jealous because I have a way with women and he hasn't!'

'He hasn't?' With a back-switch of memory Lorna recalled just how charming Wade could be. 'Your sister wouldn't agree with you, I'm afraid.'

Brock's eyes wandered to where the two were standing, having been joined by another couple, Janice and Stephen Shaw, two of the most popular members of the Outback's squatocracy, and joint owners of a huge cattle station known as Broken Rock.

'Obviously she wouldn't,' he agreed, and then, abruptly changing the subject, he asked Aunt Bertha if he could snatch Lorna away as he wanted to have another dance with her.

'Take her by all means, dear boy,' said the old lady, and waved them away.

Brock slipped an arm around her as they strolled in the direction of the brilliantly-lighted shed, from where music poured forth into the still dark bushlands.

'A barn dance.' Brock slackened his pace as he spoke. 'Strenuous. Would you rather take a stroll?'

She hesitated. She was not too comfortable, with the feel of his warm arm around her and his hand moving against her waist. Would he get fresh, out there in the lonely darkness? She could manage him, of course, simply because, once checked, he would leave her alone. His future brother-in-law's guest was not for insulting.

'I don't know, Brock. Perhaps we'd better go back to the dancing.' The truth was that she still hoped to have at least one more dance with Wade, but cherished the idea that she would have two or three. And if she

74

wasn't there she would miss the opportunity. Wade had already danced with her twice, chatting politely with her as he whirled her about in the expert manner she only too poignantly recalled. 'It might look bad – our going off alone.'

'Look bad!' he echoed, then gave a loud guffaw. 'Now why on earth should it look bad? You have an evil mind, my child, and a suspicious one. I assure you I can keep my place when necessary, so don't make silly excuses for not walking with me. Bad, indeed! Everyone goes for a walk during an evening such as this. Look, there's Wade and my sister going off into the darkness. They're bent on a little kiss and cuddle, of course, but we'll just walk, if that's what you prefer.'

Lorna's eyes followed the dark silhouettes of the two who had left everyone so as to be alone for a while. A kiss and cuddle. ... Lorna closed her eyes tightly, biting hard at her underlip to keep back the tears. Why had she come? There had been no pain like this at home – just memories, sweet and precious, of the time when Wade belonged to her for that brief and lovely spell. She had had no knowledge of his life at the present time, no inkling of whether or not he was married, or engaged. She could dream, think of him as hers still ... but now all that was gone and from this time on every memory would be of the present not the past ... and every memory would be like a sword-edge turning in her heart. She would carry memory on to imagination – yes, that was inevitable – on to the future when Olga was the proud mistress of Bali Creek, on to the time when she presented her husband with a son and heir. ...

'Yes, I do prefer to walk,' she said hastily, for it was suddenly imperative that her mind should be taken

75

into other channels, and it would be, if she walked and talked with Brock. He would draw laughter from her – forced laughter, it was true, because Lorna was sure her heart was breaking.

CHAPTER FIVE

THE darkness and immensity of the bush soon enveloped them and a strange balm resulted from the isolation so that Lorna's hurts and mental anguish were assuaged and she became possessed of a welcome peace of mind which she would never have believed possible only a short ten minutes before.

'Tell me about yourself, Lorna.' Brock was serious after having made her laugh once or twice by his witticisms. 'You're so young to be widowed. Can you talk about it?'

She twisted her head, perception in her glance.

'Aunt Bertha has told you about me,' she declared, and Brock acknowledged the truth of this by a slight inclination of his head. 'I wonder why she did? Auntie isn't usually expansive with strangers.'

Brock flicked his hand and said,

'We just happened to meet on the landing – that day I brought the students over – and I naturally showed curiosity about the reason for your both coming here. I knew of course of your coming, as Wade had told us over the air. But to me the Outback seemed an odd sort of place to take a holiday of any length and I suppose I asked a few questions. Your aunt explained that you'd had this bereavement and were very broken by the tragic loss of your husband at such an early age. She told me about her win, and her decision to take a holiday. She had always wanted to see Australia, and as Wade was an old acquaintance of hers she naturally got in touch with him, with the result that he agreed for you both to come here to stay.'

77

Both, mused Lorna, squirming at what she had overheard.

'What else did my aunt tell you?' she inquired, remembering that look of satisfaction her aunt wore after having conversed with Brock on the landing.

'Nothing much. She just said she had hopes that the holiday would do you good – would help you forget your heartbreaking loss.'

Heartbreaking loss. ... A frown fell heavily on to Lorna's brow. She had never known her aunt be so false. It was she who had always maintained that Jack's death was not only a blessed release for them both but also a timely one for Lorna. It would have been the greatest tragedy, she had said, if Jack had lived until Lorna was too old to shape her own life, to find the happiness which is everyone's birthright. Lorna herself had known a great sadness at her husband's death, but only because he was so young and had had so little from life. Never had she pretended that she was in love with her husband; Aunt Bertha had known all along that in marrying Jack Lorna had followed the dictates of her conscience and not her heart. And so it was very odd indeed that she should have used the expressions like 'heartbreaking loss' and 'broken' when speaking to Brock about the matter. There was some good reason, decided Lorna, since she had never known her aunt do anything without a good reason. What that reason was, however, Lorna had no idea. All she did know was that her aunt's behaviour recently had become more than a little puzzling; she also knew that to question Aunt Bertha would be a waste of time. She would reveal her motives only when she herself chose to do so – if at all.

'Shall we take this bush track?' Brock's low drawl cut into her reflections and she nodded. Wade and Olga had gone in the opposite direction when leaving the lights of the shed, so there was no danger of meeting them. 'I asked you to tell me about yourself?' he added after a few moments' silence.

'There's very little to tell, Brock.' But his interest, and the change from bantering frivolity to this serious – and, she admitted, soothing mood – encouraged her to talk. 'I was engaged to Jack for three years, because Father refused his consent to our marriage, and at that time a father's consent was necessary until one reached the age of twenty-one.'

'Yes, that's right.' Brock paused a moment and then, 'Three years is a long time. Many a couple would have decided to live together.'

Colour rushed to her face at this, but she found it impossible to take offence, since Brock was merely speaking practically, and probably putting himself in Jack's place.

'We weren't all that much in love,' she began, then realized that this must surely lead to some astonished questioning from Brock. 'You know how it is,' she then hastened to say, 'when you fall into a routine? The whole thing becomes – well, a sort of – habit.'

Brock looked disbelievingly at her.

'You married him, not loving him?'

She hesitated. Should she tell Brock all? It would certainly be comforting to confide in someone willing to listen and to understand. But no. She would arouse his pity, and this was the last thing she desired.

'There were other factors, Brock,' was all she would say, and the tone she used forbade any further questions on his part. However, he did say, watching her expression curiously,

'Your aunt spoke as if you were heartbrokenly mourning a dearly-loved husband.' Brock waited for

79

one hopeful moment, but when Lorna remained stubbornly silent he shrugged his shoulders and allowed the subject to drop.

The moon, now free of the clouds, showered the silent bush with its all-pervading light, while in the distance the outline of the mountains was spangled with silver. The Southern Cross added its light to the Capricornian sky; the perfumes of the natural vegetation mingled with the scent of pines clustered thickly along one side of the Norville homestead.

'I do love the peace here,' murmured Lorna, revelling in the tranquillity that had come to her during the past few moments, since they had left the lights and music and the people, most of whom were strangers to her. 'There's something fascinating about great space and silence and the absence of things which remind you of civilization. I think I would have liked to live in the days of cave-men.'

Brock laughed and said,

'You'd have been dragged along by your hair.'

Lorna responded with,

'I'd have been a savage too, remember. I'd probably have retaliated by burying my fangs in my aggressive husband's neck.'

'They didn't have husbands, only mates. You could move around from one to another; it must have been fun.'

'How like a man to think of that!'

'Don't women think of such things? I believe they do.'

'Because you want to believe it.'

'Because it's true.'

'You seem to know a lot about women.'

'I have a mother and a sister. I should know something about them. I don't go around with my eyes shut.'

'Your sister . . . how old is she?'

'Twenty-seven.' A small pause. 'How old are you?'

'Twenty-five.'

'You seem a lot younger than Olga. Perhaps it's because you're so fair and sort of – fragile.'

'I'm not fragile!'

'Sorry, my mistake.' Another pause. 'I wish you were.'

'Good gracious – why?'

'Because then you might be more approachable. I could get close enough to be able to exercise my protective instincts.'

'We're back to the cave-men again!'

'I like you, Lorna – no, I'm not flirting with you.'

'Then I don't know what flirting is!'

'Has anyone ever flirted with you, Lorna?'

'Never.'

'In that case,' he returned with a hint of triumph, 'you're quite right when you say you don't know what flirting is.'

'A point to you,' she laughed, raising her eyes to his, limpid violet eyes, filled with moonlight.

'You're a beauty!' he exclaimed, and his arm slid around her again. She tried to ease away, but failed. Brock said, in his quiet Australian voice, 'Don't be afraid, Lorna. Haven't I said I can keep my place?' She made no answer and he added in a curious tone, 'Have you ever been in love, Lorna – apart from anything you experienced, in the beginning, for your husband?'

Lorna felt the colour leave her face. She said, her vision presenting a picture of Wade, out here, somewhere not too far away, holding Olga in his arms . . .

81

kissing her with those hard demanding lips, pressing her body to him . . . inciting her with ardour,

'Once, yes.'

'Tell me about it.'

She shook her head.

'It's my own precious secret, Brock, so please – no inquisitive questions.'

'I'll respect your wish,' he said seriously, 'even though I'm all agog with curiosity.'

'Tell me about yourself,' she invited. 'Why haven't you found someone to go steady with before now?'

'What do you mean, before now? I'm only twenty-nine and a bit!'

'Well, you're past the chicken stage. You ought to be getting married. Don't you ever think about an heir?'

'I suppose one has to think about an heir, and I expect I shall do something about it before very long. I'd rather marry for love, though; I'm not the cold unemotional sort that can look at marriage as a business venture. I might be a flirt, as Wade asserted, but when the time comes for marrying all that will be over – in the past. Marriage is something I want to acquire for keeps.'

His grave and sincerely-spoken words startled her a little. She had not suspected him of a seriousness quite so deep as this.

'I suppose,' she said after a while, 'that your choice is limited – here, in the Outback?'

'To a certain extent it is,' he agreed. 'I have friends in Brisbane, though, and I go for breaks now and then. One of these days I shall find myself a bride, I expect.' He paused a moment, thoughtfully. 'Wade surprised us all – getting engaged to my sister at last.'

'At last?' Lorna glanced around. They had lost the

shed lights, also those of the Norville homestead, but she supposed Brock knew where he was going.

'Olga's been after him since she was about twenty. It's no secret, so I'm not telling tales out of school,' Brock added hastily as he sensed his companion's surprise. 'He wouldn't look at her and she used to get so mad. Then, about four years ago, he went off to England to look up some relatives and he met a girl there—'

'He met a girl!' The interruption came swiftly, involuntarily, and Brock looked interrogatingly at her.

'Yes . . . is something wrong?'

'No – no, of course not. Do go on.'

'He didn't tell any of us he'd met this girl, but one day not long after his return, he was fishing something out of his wallet and a snapshot fell on to the floor. It was at a party and Wade's mother was alive then. She picked it up; Olga and I were standing close, but they didn't notice us, as there were lots of people around. We heard Mrs. Harcourt asking about this girl. Wade had been very strange since returning from his visit to England – sort of morose, and hadn't any patience with anyone. His mother wanted to know who the girl was and at first Wade was non-committal, but he thought a lot of his mother and after a while he said he had met this girl in England and they'd been going about together. Well, you know what mothers are – she wanted to know more, and she asked him outright if he'd fallen in love with this pommy and he said yes, he had.'

'Wade told his mother that?' Lorna wondered if she were as white as she felt, and was glad of the dimness which to some extent hid her face.

'She forced it from him. Of course, she asked more questions, but he refused to answer – although I think he might have told her more later, when they were alone. There was no doubt that he was quite haggard when he was telling his mother about this girl, and it was not difficult to see that whatever had transpired the fact that she didn't marry him practically broke him up.'

Broke him up. ... Lorna's heart contracted. That she should have hurt him so, he whom she had worshipped, who had meant more to her than life itself. Lorna knew in this moment of desolation that had she her time to come over again she would not make the same decision. Wade would come first – before conscience, duty or compassion.

'The snapshot,' she whispered, recalling that Wade had taken so many of her. 'No one saw it, I suppose, other than his mother?'

Brock had not expected this question; Lorna saw that at once, for he turned his head from her and she sensed a sudden shame sweeping over him.

'Not then, because of course Wade had taken it from his mother's hand immediately she picked it up. All she had time for was a glance before it was back in her son's wallet. But—' He broke off and Lorna said pressingly,

'But what, Brock?'

'I hate to admit it, Lorna, but my sister had a look at it, unknown to Wade—'

'She looked at it?' So much was explained now – the start which Olga had given on first being introduced to Lorna, the odd inflection in her voice, the undisguised hostility. 'How could she see it, unknown to Wade?'

'She – she took out the wallet from his pocket – when his coat was hanging on a peg in the hall. We were at a party, remember, and it was a very warm night. We all took our coats off.' Brock stopped in the track and

84

turned to her. 'I shouldn't have told you this – you, a stranger! Forget it, Lorna – promise me!'

'Yes. ...' She spoke almost inaudibly. Olga knew that she was the girl Wade had once been in love with ... 'Yes, Brock, I'll forget it – I mean, I'll never repeat it to anyone, if that's what you mean?'

'Thanks, Lorna.' He breathed a great sigh and began strolling on again. 'As I said, Olga wanted Wade from about the time she was twenty. She was furious on learning of this girl, and especially as Wade still wouldn't look at her despite the fact that the affair with this pommy had fizzled out and died almost before it was born. He'd been hard hit, though, you could see it for a long while. But eventually he recovered – it was inevitable, as no one can go on pining for ever. And at last he began taking notice of Olga, and about a couple of months ago they got engaged.'

'He – he loves her now, you think?' Lorna had not meant to say a thing like that and once again she was glad that it wasn't too light, for she had coloured with embarrassment and she would not have cared for Brock to see this. 'I'm sorry; that wasn't quite the thing to say. Wade must love her, naturally.'

To her surprise Brock paused a while before saying, with a slight shrug which could have been meant to convey either indifference or agreement,

'I expect he does love her, otherwise he wouldn't be marrying her.' He stopped again and glanced at his wrist watch. 'It can't be—!' He moved the face until it caught the moonlight at an angle. 'Lord, it'll all be over by the time we get back! I'd no idea it was so late. And we've come the devil of a way!'

It was not over when they reached the shed again, but they had been gone for over an hour and a half and the first thing Wade said to them was,

85

'Some of us thought you'd got lost.' His keen grey eyes settled on Lorna's face, flushed because she had been hurrying. 'Did you enjoy your . . . walk?' Biting tones, and she smarted under them; her colour increased and she suddenly wanted desperately to find comfort in tears. She blinked rapidly and her mouth quivered. Why should she care what Wade thought about her? His love was transferred to someone else; he was soon to be married, so why did his opinion of her matter so much? In a few weeks at most she would be gone from here, and she and Wade would never meet again. She touched her throat automatically, aware that she and Wade were quite alone, on the softly-illuminated verandah of the huge wooden shed, Brock having gone off inside to dance with one of his mother's home helps.

'Yes, thank you, Wade, I did enjoy my walk.'

'You must have gone a long way?'

She nodded and said,

'It was a long way, yes.'

Wade looked down at her and she stared into his eyes, her fingers still pressed to her throat, for a lump had settled there.

'You'll be too tired to dance, I expect?'

Her colour fluctuated; the limpid violet eyes withheld their secret from him with difficulty. Up till now she had managed very well to keep from Wade the fact that she still cared, spurred to even greater effort by the fact of her aunt's suggesting to Wade that he and her niece could begin all over again. Fortunately he believed the idea was all Aunt Bertha's, and that Lorna herself was in ignorance of what the old lady had had in mind when embarking on this trip.

'I'm not tired,' she told Wade softly at last, and without another word he took her arm and led her into

86

the gay company inside the shed. With ease and effortless movement he guided her among the dancers, his figure just that bit taller even than that of Brock, who was laughing gaily with his partner.

'Did you have to fight off Brock's amorous inclinations?' The voice was tight, the smile thin and automatic. Lorna kept her head raised, meeting the question in those metallic grey eyes. 'I seem to remember you were quite confident about being able to deal with him.'

'I didn't have to deal with him. He was entirely the gentleman.'

'All that time?' The implication should by rights have angered, but it only hurt.

'We talked, Wade, and – and strolled along. Brock made no advances.' Her voice was low and husky, but it was the voice of truth, the frank sweet voice he had once known and loved. She seemed to feel his hard body stiffen and thought it was at some persistent memory. She felt a closeness despite his withdrawal; it was a strange unfathomable sensation, but one which she wished fervently to prolong.

'Obviously Brock respects my guests,' was all Wade said, and the subject was closed. 'Your aunt wants to accompany me to Yarralinga on Monday,' he told Lorna when presently the music stopped and he and she went out to the verandah again. 'Are you coming too?'

Her eyes brightened.

'I'd love to. Thank you for asking me.' Her eagerness sprang forth, bringing a glow to her eyes. Wade's tongue passed over his lips; his throat seemed blocked when he swallowed. Then his mouth tightened and she was a long, long way from him and his remoteness hurt and chilled and brought tears into her lovely eyes.

87

'There isn't a lot to see there, Lorna. Just the bank and a few offices and shops, and a couple of eating places, of course.'

'It'll be something unusual; I'll thoroughly enjoy it.'

He looked at her, broodingly. She noted the harshness about his mouth, the brittle light that had never been in his eyes during those happy days of long ago. Tenderness, softness and adoration she had seen, but never the hardness that was almost always in evidence now. What was he like when he and Olga were alone? Somehow – perhaps because she did not want to – Lorna could not imagine his being anywhere near so loving and tender with his fiancée as he had been with her. Ardent, yes, decided Lorna, for Olga was undoubtedly the type to arouse passion and desire in a man – with her dark exotic beauty, her full inviting lips, and her figure. . . .

'The Alice is the real place for tourists,' he said at last. 'Perhaps we must see that you and your aunt visit it before you return to England.'

'You'll take us – in the aeroplane?' Her eagerness returned, but was checked a little. Wade was still a long way off.

'I could manage it, I think. We'll see, Lorna. If I can find the time I'll take you – just for a couple of days or so.' He turned as Aunt Bertha appeared, flushed and breathless.

'My, but I do hope I've lost a bit of weight during the past hour or two – otherwise it won't have been worth it!'

'You mean,' said Wade in some amusement, 'that you dance only with the idea of slimming in view?'

'At my age, yes!' She moved a little closer to her niece. 'I saw you going off with that charming Brock.

88

Did you have a nice stroll, dear?'

'Very enjoyable, Auntie.'

'He's so attractive – don't you think so, Wade?'

'I expect he does appeal to the ladies,' he conceded in a dry and casual tone.

'And when he was dancing with you, Lorna – you were without doubt the most striking couple on the floor – Oh, forgive me, Wade! You and your very charming fiancée also attracted a good deal of attention.' Aunt Bertha stopped for breath and Lorna looked oddly at her. Charming fiancée. . . . After stating so emphatically how much she disliked the girl. Aunt Bertha had never before shown hypocritical tendencies. 'Yes, you and Brock certainly looked a well-matched couple. Don't you agree, Wade?' she said, turning to him.

'I didn't notice, Mrs. Gerrard.'

'No? Then do, the next time they're together—'

'Auntie,' cut in Lorna, unable to allow her to continue like this, 'it isn't at all important what Brock and I look like when we're dancing together. Sit down, pet, you look exhausted.'

'Thanks, dear. Yes, it is tiring, all that dancing around. Mind you, I managed very well. That young David thought I'd give up, during that barn dance, but I didn't – not likely!'

Wade laughed; it eased the situation for Lorna, who had been embarrassed by her aunt's talk. And Wade from then on seemed in a more mellowed mood, leaning back against a stout wooden pillar and chatting casually to his two guests. Richard came out and, seeing Lorna, immediately claimed her for a dance. Stuart and the doctor also danced with her, also Robert Mowbray, whom she liked enormously. Wade had come back and had a couple of dances with his fiancée, and then he came over to Lorna again.

'Shall we dance?' he asked, anticipating her readiness by extending an open palm. Lorna put hers on to it and thrilled to the feel of his fingers curling round the back of her hand. To him it was an automatic action, one which would have applied to any girl whom he happened to be taking on to the dance floor, but to Lorna it was another precious memory added to her slowly-mounting store. 'Have you enjoyed yourself?' he inquired, and she nodded enthusiastically. 'I've loved every minute of it!'

'Every minute. . . .' He seemed to take a deep breath and his head turned. Brock came under his attention; words rose to his lips as Lorna watched his face, but the next second his features relaxed, as if the words were suppressed by some inner compulsion. He had intended making some remark about her stroll with Brock, she knew, and she felt instinctively that it would have carried an element of sarcasm. But he had held it back, and Lorna knew a great swell of happiness at this sudden decision to spare her feelings.

But her happiness was damped all at once as she caught Olga's expression. She was dancing with her brother, and as they came alongside Wade and Lorna, Olga's face went tight with anger as she noted Lorna's rather glowing countenance. Wade, unnoticing, bent his head to say something to his partner; Olga's mouth compressed into an ugly line and the dark eyes glittered. Was she afraid? The idea staggered Lorna since it could mean that despite the engagement Olga was not entirely sure of Wade. No, this could not be the case, Lorna decided. What Olga felt was merely jealousy – the natural jealousy that could be expected in a person of her type on discovering that Wade was entertaining as a guest the girl with whom he had once been in love.

'I think I would perhaps also feel a tinge of jealousy were it to happen to me,' Lorna said to herself. But not by any stretch of imagination could she visualize herself harbouring such open hostility as that which was without doubt consuming Olga at the present time.

CHAPTER SIX

MANY of the guests had to stay the night at the Norville homestead, but Wade had decided to drive home, much to the disappointment of his fiancée who had asked him to change his mind and stay.

'I'm sorry, Olga, but we're exceedingly busy at Bali Creek at the present time. We've several thousand clearskins to be brought in for branding—'

'But you needn't work. You've plenty of stockmen to bring them in.'

He shook his head firmly. Lorna, standing not too far from where the couple were talking, remembered that expression and she was surprised to hear Olga continue her persuasions, for she must also be aware of what that set look portended. Wade in this mood would brook no argument and had Lorna been in Olga's shoes she would immediately have desisted from any further attempts to make him change his mind about going home.

'I like to be on hand, Olga.'

'It isn't necessary, darling. Please stay. We don't see very much of one another. I won't *let* you go home until tomorrow!'

'What's up with Sis?' Brock's voice was a whisper in Lorna's ear and she turned, unaware that he had come up to her. 'Can't she see she's fighting a losing battle? If Wade says he's for home then he's for home and that's that.'

'You won't let me?' Wade's soft Australian drawl was edged with ice suddenly. 'Is that what you said, Olga?

92

His fiancée coloured; Lorna noticed one of her fists was clenched tightly at her side.

'You're most unkind not to pander to me, Wade,' she said with a pout that was meant to be pretty, Lorna felt sure, but which was in fact the opposite. It had no effect on Wade whatsoever, nor had her protest, apparently, for he totally ignored it.

'I'll see you next Thursday at the barbecue. And now, Olga, I must be getting along. It'll be going on for three o'clock before we get home.'

Again Olga pouted. She said querulously,

'We've plenty of room for you all to stay, so why drive over a hundred miles at this time of the night? I'm sure the others don't want to go back to Bali Creek at this late hour.'

'She never seems to learn,' whispered Brock with a grin. 'He'll teach her once he has her married!'

Wade had seen them and, leaving Olga, he approached them.

'Lorna, I believe your aunt is ready. I'm going now.'

'Yes.' She smiled at Brock. 'Good night – or is it morning? You'll be coming to Wade's barbecue?'

'Bet your life I shall. I can't wait to see you again. In fact,' he added thoughtfully, and oblivious of Wade's impatient frown, 'I think I'll come over on Monday, just to look you up, as it were.'

'We're going into town on Monday, Brock,' Wade told him quietly, 'so it won't be any good your coming.'

'To town?' from Olga, who had followed Wade and was now standing at his side, her hand on his sleeve, possessively. 'You're taking Mrs. Trent and her aunt?'

'That's right. I have business at the bank and they

93

might as well come with me.' He glanced at his watch. Olga pursed her lips in a gesture of anger, but the only response she dared offer was a shrug and a rather chill,

'Good night, Wade, until the barbecue.'

She came with Wade and his party to the car, but no further words were spoken between her and her fiancé, and on casting Wade a sideways glance as she sat beside him in the dimness of the car, Lorna could not help noticing the set of his mouth and the tautness of his jaw. And for the whole of the homeward journey he scarcely spoke, merely answering Aunt Bertha or one or other of the students, should they put a question to him. As for Lorna herself, she soon began to doze, but on coming to with a start as Wade braked to avoid a dingo which was crossing the road, and finding that her head had come to rest against his shoulder, she determinedly kept herself awake until they arrived back at the homestead.

The following morning the jacko wakened her as usual; his mate soon appeared and Lorna was afforded the familiar entertainment of watching them enjoy the breakfast which Dinah had brought out to them. Her eyes wandered towards the mountains, sun-touched in parts but in other parts subtly shaded with tints of purple through to heliotrope, and with soft patches of pink here and there so that the entire mass lost its gaunt aspect of austerity and became gentle under the influence of the sunrise. Lorna gave a small sigh. She would miss it all when the time for leaving arrived, as very soon it must. She had grown used to waking each morning to a world which was a revelation of almost unearthly beauty. The magic of light, spreading as the sun rose higher in the sky, cast an ever-changing aspect to the scene and sometimes the wide and boundless

94

spinifex plains would become an opalescent wonder of changing colour – crimson to carmine, red-ochre to fiery pink, while away on the marginal edges of her vision cattle silhouettes stood darkly defined against the Capricornian skyline.

Her aunt was not getting up for breakfast, Lorna learned on entering the room from where there came the delicious and appetising smell of bacon and eggs and coffee.

'I didn't expect to see you either.' Wade, dressed in tight jeans and a plain brown cotton shirt, regarded Lorna's face critically as if he would ascertain whether or not she was showing evidence of lack of sleep. 'Didn't you feel like a lie-in?'

'The jacko woke me,' she smiled. 'In any case, I like to see the sunrise.'

Wade pulled out a chair for her and she sat down.

'Your aunt seems to enjoy having her breakfast in bed. Is this usual or merely a departure since coming here?'

'She's never done it before – at least, not since I came to live with her. She always insists on getting up to make my breakfast, even though I'm against it, for it's so unnecessary. I can manage very well to get myself a cup of coffee and some toast.' She was puzzled in the extreme by her aunt's regular non-appearance at the breakfast table. This morning was understandable, as they had arrived back at Bali Creek in the early hours, but for the rest – Lorna had been becoming more and more puzzled as time went on, for her aunt had put in an appearance on just a couple of occasions, and that only in the beginning.

Wade sat down opposite to Lorna, his face thoughtful.

'You were fortunate in having your aunt to go to

95

when your – husband died,' he commented, helping himself to toast and taking a pat of butter from the dish which Lorna had picked up and was holding out to him. The noticeable hesitation before he mentioned her husband brought a hint of dejection to her, for the circumstance seemed to result in a certain reserve settling on him, and a dignity that was, somehow, protective. Was he recalling the bitter hurt she had inflicted on him? Surely not, after all this time, and when he was now engaged to someone else.

'I was, yes,' she replied, wondering how much her aunt had told him about her. She was not to be left guessing for long. Wade said, mechanically spreading butter over his toast,

'You were turned out of your home, your aunt was telling me?'

Lorna nodded her head. The sunlight, streaming in through the wide window, caught her hair in its flattering golden rays, and Wade swallowed and frowned and lowered his eyes to his plate.

'The house belonged to my brother-in-law. He wanted to sell it, naturally.'

'Naturally!' It was an unchecked exclamation, impelled by indignation. 'I find it far from natural for anyone to wish to put another person out of her home.'

Lorna eyed him curiously. Was that pity she detected in his tone? Pity. . . . The word had a wounding effect. Pity was the very last thing she desired from Wade. It would be too unbearable to live with the knowledge that she had his pity while another girl had his love.

'I'm exceedingly happy with my aunt,' she assured him, forcing a bright smile. 'We're good company for one another. I know now it was for the best – my

96

having to give up my home, I mean – because I shall always be on hand if ever Auntie is ill, or when the time comes when she's unable to look after herself.'

Wade's mouth went tight. He held out a silver dish, silently inviting Lorna to help herself to bacon and eggs.

'You're resigned to spending your life with her?' He spoke after a long interval of silence during which he had been lost in thought.

'Yes – yes, I am,' she replied, adding a thank-you when she had taken what she wanted from the dish.

He fell strangely silent then, but surprised her later when on finishing his breakfast he said,

'I'm riding over to one of the bore-troughs; it's developed a fault and I want to see what's gone wrong. Would you care to ride with me? It isn't going to be pleasant for you, staying here on your own. I expect your aunt will be up by the time we get back and then you'll have company.'

The word pity leapt to her mind again and she was instantly conscious of a protective armour enclosing her. But despite this the temptation was too great for her and she scarcely hesitated at all before saying,

'I'd love to, Wade.'

'Come along then, and we'll have Juno saddled.'

His own horse was ready and he took the reins from Simon, who on hearing Wade's request went off immediately to saddle the mare who, used to Lorna by now, whinneyed on seeing her. A smile broke over Lorna's features and her eyes shone.

'She knows me,' she said, looking happily up at Wade.

'She'll miss you when you go,' put in Simon, scratching his head in a gesture he had. 'Horses get attached to people – you know that, don't you, Boss?'

Wade nodded but made no reply. Giving Lorna his hand, he helped her up and she thanked him with a smile, her face aglow because of the happiness within her and the fact that Olga was over a hundred miles away and she, Lorna, had Wade's company all to herself for a precious hour or two.

The ascent of the sun gave added colour to the lonely, lovely rangelands which became a polychromic wonder of mauve and gold and vivid shades of green. The waving heads of spinifex grass stretched into infinity, the soils that gave them support having been born of the ancient Mesozoic and Paleozoic sediments which must in those far-off times of pre-history have assumed the aspect of a boundless and terrifying wilderness, hostile and unconquerable.

As they rode side by side Lorna cast a glance at the silent man whose face was set and stern, whose figure, upright and carrying not an ounce of unnecessary weight, seemed to be one with the magnificent animal he rode. Despite her determination to regard him merely as someone she had known in the past but who was now no more than a casual friend, Lorna knew a quickening of her pulse and her heart throbbed with the consciousness of her love for him. From the moment of meeting after all that time his attractiveness had remained disturbingly in her thoughts. She had pondered sometimes, during the past couple of weeks, whether his welcome would have been warmer had he not been engaged to someone else. But no, for hadn't he told Aunt Bertha in his letter that Lorna would not be welcome at Bali Creek? The truth was, Lorna felt sure, that he could never forgive her for the hurt she had caused him. This meant that even had he had no ties he would never have had any desire to begin again with the girl who had sent him away, carrying with

98

him the heartbreaking knowledge that she was shortly to marry another man. It was understandable that he found it impossible to forgive her.

'You're not getting tired?' Wade's question came after they had been jogging along for a while.

'No. I'm enjoying it enormously!' She stopped abruptly after uttering the exclamation; Wade had seemed to tug at the reins, for his mount reared a little, in surprise. Leaning forward, Wade patted its neck, a gesture of apology, silent, but understood by the horse. Wade turned his head and Lorna knew by his expression that, like her, he had been struck by a matching memory, the memory that had caused her to cut off abruptly after saying she was enjoying it enormously.

Long ago, he had crushed her so tightly to him that he had her breathless and, she had felt sure, rather more than a little bruised.

'Beloved,' he had said contritely, 'am I hurting you?'

'No,' had come the eager response, 'I'm enjoying it enormously!'

And he had remembered ... after all this time. . . .

'We'll be in time to join some of the men for smoko,' he said a little brusquely. 'I expect you could do with a drink?'

'A cup of tea would be nice.' Her voice caught, so that her accents faltered. Wade returned his gaze to the scene ahead, where his cattle grazed the green slopes and stockriders moved about in their midst.

He took a look at the bore-trough first, frowning at the state of the water.

'I'll get someone along to see to it,' he told Luke, his head stockman. 'In the meantime, keep the cattle

99

away.'

'Yes, I've already given orders regarding that.' Luke surveyed Lorna with interest. He had seen the couple approaching at a leisurely trot, and had watched them curiously, surprised that the Boss of Bali Creek would take so slow a pace. 'Are you staying for a drink?'

'Of course,' replied Wade.

He tethered Gladiator while Luke secured Juno.

'Have a seat,' he invited, indicating a small flat-topped boulder.

'Thank you.' She smiled up at him as she sat down, conscious of other eyes fixed upon her, curious eyes, which moved now and then from her to the man who had brought her here. He was leaning against a tree, his slouch hat pushed to the back of his head. The sunlight caught the lighter shades of his hair and brought it into contrast with the deep bronze of his skin.

One of the Aboriginal stockmen was squatting over the billy; others stood around, their horses tethered, waiting for a drink. Lorna allowed her eyes to stray. These few humans, she thought, in all this vast expanse of land, and she thought of the crowds of people in the town in which she worked, crowds of busy men and women scurrying about like an army of ants ... going where ...? No time to stop for a chat, no time to look about them, seeking for the beauty of trees still left, or to glance up and appreciate the pretty window box someone had lovingly planted with colourful blooms. In fact, all those scurrying little human ants had so cluttered up their lives with non-essentials that there was time only for this race towards the goal that was never reached. Certainly there was no time at all to 'stand and stare'.

Here the pace was slow, the comradeship strong;

100

there was space in plenty, fresh pure air and the beauties of nature to be enjoyed.

'What thoughts are occupying you so intently that you frown one moment and faintly smile the next?' Wade's voice drifting to her from where he stood, in a sort of careless abandon, by the tree. One hand was tucked into his belt, the other absently stroking his chin. She looked at him, the smile still hovering on her lips. Her hat was pushed back from her forehead, her checked shirt open at the neck.

'I was thinking of the vast difference in my environment and yours. At home we're all so crowded; we live in little boxes, identical but for the trimmings. . . .' She trailed off to silence as Wade raised his eyebrows. A soft flush of colour touched her cheeks, enchantingly. Her mouth quivered, because Wade was now evidencing some amusement and she was only too ready to respond since here was another memory to add to her little store.

'You . . . prefer it here?' Slow the tones and husky with the typical Australian accent. A strangeness stole over Lorna; she was unable to explain her tingling senses or the swell of emotion that rose within her. She answered truthfully,

'Yes, I do prefer it here. I love the peace, and space—' She stopped, brought up sharply by the memory that she had already said this to him on a previous occasion when they had been out riding in the bush; and she naturally recalled also the invidious words of Olga's – words which Wade at first believed, but was later to know had in fact been lies.

'Then you'll have to stay,' from Luke as he handed her a mug of tea. 'The Boss will find you a job. We're always wanting willing hands. Can you cook?' he asked with a grin. Others were listening; they too grinned, and Lorna gave them a second's attention. Big husky Outback men all, with ravenous appetites, she had heard from Dinah who, with a couple of gins, looked to all the food the men ate. Great masses of beefsteaks were cooked every day; the men even ate meat for breakfast.

'I could never cook in the quantities required by so many hungry men,' she said with a laugh. 'I only cook for my aunt and myself, and that not very often – just at week-ends sometimes.'

Wade was still watching her; she strove to appear cool and collected, but the way he had spoken a few moments ago still affected her, for there seemed to be something far deeper than the question suggested.

'You really are pleasantly surprised by our country, it would appear.' Again that suggestion of a deeper current. Lorna felt the necessity to adopt a guarded manner, although she could not have said why.

'It more than comes up to my expectations,' she replied truthfully. 'I like the idea of living close to nature, you see.' Her voice was light, the emotion encompassing her being kept firmly out of her voice.

'We certainly live close to nature here,' said Luke, giving Wade his tea. 'How about the fun and lights? Surely you miss them a little?'

Lorna shook her head.

'There are so many compensations. I'd rather walk in the evenings than dance.'

'But you enjoyed the shed dance?'

'Yes, of course. That again was different, though. It was more exciting than a dance hall.'

One or two of the men grimaced.

'I wouldn't mind a visit to a dance hall now and then,' said Kip, one of the youngest of the stockriders. 'I wouldn't change, though,' he added as Wade threw him a glance. 'I've never been used to a city and I don't think I ever could get used to one.'

'You've always lived here, at Bali Creek?'

'That's right; I was born here. My dad came here as a young rouseabout when Mr. Harcourt's father was the boss.' He took a long drink and held out his mug for the Aboriginal stockman to refill it. 'It's a good life, and a healthy one.'

Having drunk his tea Wade looked at Lorna.

'Ready?' he asked, and she drank up quickly, handed her mug to Luke and a moment or two later she and Wade were cantering over the plain towards the homestead, sheltered and hidden behind the belt of ghost gums and other trees of the Inland.

Aunt Bertha was on the verandah when they arrived and she watched their approach through narrowed eyes.

'You've been riding with Wade?' she said when, having left him at the saddling paddock, Lorna came with light and springing steps across the lawn to join her.

'It was lovely! We've been riding for nearly three hours — with a break for smoko in between. We had it with the men, out there on the range.' She was flushed and happy, forgetting everything except the fact that she had come a little closer to Wade during that ride; she knew that she was no longer an unwelcome guest in his home. If only he could forgive her before she left Bali Creek for ever, Lorna felt she could more easily face the long lonely future that she knew was hers. Before coming here she had sometimes wondered if in the distant future she would remarry, but now she was resigned to the fact that this was impossible.

Aunt Bertha was nodding her head thoughtfully. She seemed preoccupied, and Lorna sat down, her eyes wandering to the horseman who was riding off again, in another direction from that which he and Lorna had taken earlier. There were numerous calves to be brought in for branding, as he had told his fiancée, and now he was about to set the operation in motion.

'What made Wade decide to ride with you?' Aunt Bertha inquired at last, her eyes following the direction of her niece's gaze. 'He's usually so busy, especially early in the morning, when it's cool and fresh.'

'It was because you were in bed. He thought I'd be lonely on my own.'

The pale blue eyes widened. Aunt Bertha began nodding again and Lorna frowned at the action. Wade disappeared from view and Aunt Bertha brought her eyes to her niece's face.

'That was very thoughtful of him,' she commented, without much expression, and Lorna's frown deepened slightly. There was no doubt about it, Aunt Bertha was not quite herself lately. There was something strange about her, and the preoccupation Lorna had noticed was becoming almost a regular occurrence. Quite often she would drift away, as if some most vital matter were occupying her mind.

'He was going to examine a faulty bore-trough,' Lorna explained, 'and he said I might as well ride along with him.'

'That was very thoughtful of him,' murmured Aunt Bertha, apparently unaware that she had made this pronouncement only seconds before.

'You do act in the oddest way,' Lorna could not help saying. 'Have you anything on your mind, Auntie?'

Startled by the question, her aunt shook her head vigorously . . . too vigorously, thought Lorna, waiting with interest for her reply.

'Of course I haven't anything on my mind, child.

Whatever made you ask a question like that?'

'It's the way you are,' returned Lorna vaguely.

'The way I am?'

'I can't explain – exactly. But you're not your usual self.'

Her aunt frowned at her, but Lorna eyed her suspiciously, sure that her puzzlement was assumed.

'You're imagining things, dear,' was all she said, and changed the subject. 'I'm very much looking forward to going to Yarralinga, aren't you?'

'Yes.' Lorna paused a moment, watching a lizard cautiously emerging from behind a flower-pot. 'Wade says too that he might find the time to take us to Alice Springs.'

'He did?' with surprise. 'I should have thought he'd be too busy for anything in the nature of a pleasure trip.'

Lorna remained quiet for a moment and then,

'When are you thinking of going home, Auntie?'

The old woman looked at her profile, an odd expression in her eyes.

'Do you want to go home?'

'Not really. . . .'

'Not really? What exactly do you mean by that?'

It was too difficult to explain, and Lorna sat in thoughtful silence. Her aunt said presently,

'You're still in love with him, aren't you, Lorna?'

'No – I've told you I'm not. It – it was all so different, once I'd met Wade again—' Lorna broke off. Observing those watchful eyes she could no longer be sure that her aunt had been successfully deceived. At first she was, undoubtedly, but Lorna sensed that she had since guessed the truth – that she, Lorna, had denied being in love with Wade merely in order to put her aunt's conscience at rest. And yet, mused Lorna with a frown, if Aunt Bertha *were* now in possession of the truth then surely she would be showing some signs of guilt at having brought her niece here to Bali Creek, telling her optimistically that she and Wade could begin all over again. There was not the merest hint of guilt or contrition about her, and with a little impatient shrug Lorna put the vexing matter from her, deciding that her aunt was becoming something of an enigma since her arrival at Bali Creek.

The following day, Sunday, Brock came on the air and asked for Lorna. Wade brought the message, looking rather formidable as he passed it on to Lorna, who was sunbathing on the lawn, her aunt having decided to take a nap after lunch.

'He wants me?' Rising, she reached for a wrap and draped it around her shoulders.

'For you,' tersely, and as she moved away, drawing together the edges of her wrap as she did so, Lorna was profoundly conscious of his eyes following her right up to the moment of her entering the house.

'Hi—!' was Brock's boisterous greeting. 'How's the fair Lorna today?'

She laughed.

'Fine – but why do you want to speak to me?'

'Do I have to give an excuse?'

'Well, no, but I fail to see—'

'I merely wanted a chat. What were you doing a couple of minutes ago?'

'Sunbathing.'

'What in?'

'In?' she repeated. 'On, you mean? I was on the lawn.'

'Obtuse maiden – I meant what I said. What in?' Lorna sought for words and he added, 'Was it a mere scrap of tantalizing cover top and – er – lower?'

She coloured, but managed to match her tones to his own flippancy.

'I had on a bikini, yes.'

'Had?' he echoed roguishly.

'It's still on, but covered most adequately with a wrap.'

'Could I have been there before you donned it!'

'You're flirting with me, Brock. Wade warned me about you, remember?'

'Oh, him! And do you heed all he says to you?'

'He's my host.'

'Ah, that you were *my* guest!'

'Would I be safe?' she challenged, laughing.

'If you wanted to be safe – yes.' A small pause and then, 'Lorna—' with sudden earnestness '—I'm going to Brisbane in about a week's time. Will you fly with me? I'm going to visit my grandmother and two of my cousins who live with her. I'd like your company, and you'd like my grandmother.'

An uneasy silence followed while Lorna pondered just how to phrase a diplomatic refusal. Failing to do so, she stalled with,

'I'll consult Auntie and see how she feels—'

'I wasn't inviting Auntie; I was inviting you. We'd stay with my relatives for about three or four days. I could show you around and we could dance and do a show or two in the evenings. Think about it, Lorna – promise?'

'I don't know, Brock. . . .'

'You'd be as safe as you are with Wade. I can't say any more than that, can I?'

'I'm quite sure I'd be safe, Brock. It's silly to bring anything like that into it. But I couldn't leave my aunt.'

'You'd like to?'

107

'No, I don't think I would.' There was no way of practising tact, it seemed, for Brock was not intending easily to be put off. 'Thank you for asking me,' she added swiftly as she thought she detected a sigh of impatience coming over the air, 'but I really must refuse.'

And now she definitely did hear a sigh.

'You're off to Yarralinga tomorrow morning?'

'That's right.'

'Looking forward to it?'

'Naturally.'

A strange pause and then, slowly and so softly that Lorna had to strain her ear to catch the words,

'It may or may not interest you to know that my sister's jealous of you.'

'Jealous?' Lorna's voice was more than a little unsteady. 'What on earth do you mean, Brock?'

'Oh, you know what women are. She just doesn't like the idea of another girl – and an exceedingly pretty one at that – living in the house of her fiancé. I suppose it's natural.'

Lorna recalled that she herself had owned that she wouldn't have liked the idea of an old flame of her fiancé's being his guest. And of course, Olga knew that she was the girl with whom Wade had once been in love. Brock on the other hand was in ignorance of the tenseness of the situation and Lorna said,

'Has Olga said something to you about not liking the idea of my being at Bali Creek?'

'Not in so many words, but it's not difficult to read her; I've been doing it for years, just for amusement. She just hated the idea of his riding with you, and she's not at all pleased about this trip to town.' Lorna said nothing and he added rather urgently, 'You'll never let this out? I mean, it's all in confidence. But I just thought I'd mention it to you – don't really know why.'

'I'll not say anything,' she promised, amazed that Brock should divulge his sister's jealousy like this.

'Where's Wade now?'

'I don't know. He was in the garden a few minutes ago.'

'He's got the barbecue all arranged, I suppose?'

'I think so. Simon was busy fixing lanterns in the trees, and Dinah and the two gins were having a little good-natured grouse about all the extra work.'

'I don't know why; they'll have plenty of help, if I know Wade. None of us gives quite as much consideration to our employees as he does. I don't know how those women'll go on when they get Olga for a mistress; she does enjoy giving ours a demonstration of her superiority.'

Lorna frowned; she disliked intensely these disparaging references to his sister. They seemed to be made without prior thought, but that was no excuse.

'I think I'd better go now, Brock. It must be getting near teatime, and I have to bath and dress.'

'Okay. See you at the barbecue. 'Bye, my lovely!'

Nerves tingling suddenly, Lorna turned to see Wade standing there, his face set and that firm square jaw flexed and taut.

'What did our Don Juan want to say to you that was so important?' In Wade's brusque inquiry there was a hint of sardonic amusement, although no trace of humour was reflected in the look he gave her.

'He merely wanted to have a chat.' Lorna looked apologetically at him. 'You didn't mind?'

'Mind?' with brows upraised. 'Why should I?'

'You – you seem – annoyed?' Lorna bent her head, because his expression hurt. Her fair hair fell forward on to her face, enchantingly protective. Wade contemplated her for a long while, deep in thought. At last she said, out of the pregnant hush that had grown between them, 'Are you annoyed with me, Wade?'

'What right have I to be annoyed?' he queried unexpectedly. 'You must do what you like ... but I *have* warned you about Brock,' he added, and Lorna knew for sure that these words of caution had been the result of some compulsion within him.

'Brock knows his place,' she told Wade quietly.

'Why did he want to speak to you – or is it a private matter?'

'As I said, he merely wanted a chat.' Caution sealed her lips regarding the invitation she had received, but only for a moment. Scanning Wade's face, she reached the conclusion that he had heard at least part of her conversation with Brock. 'He asked me to go to Brisbane with him. He's visiting his grandmother,' she added on seeing Wade's mouth tighten. Why this keen interest? she asked herself. After treating her with noticeable indifference at first, he was now betraying an inordinate amount of interest in her.

'And are you going?'

Lorna shook her head.

'No, I told him I couldn't leave Auntie—' She stopped, angry with herself at the lack of presence of mind that had been responsible for this all-revealing statement. Wade looked hard at her, his mouth set.

'He wanted you to go alone?'

Lorna moistened her lips. Why this tinge of fear? She had known fear before – fear of Wade – but it was the exquisite kind, with expectations of a tender scene to follow. Now, however, it was real trepidation she experienced, and it caused her heartbeats to quicken almost painfully.

110

'He did suggest we go alone, yes,' she had to admit, noting the darkling expression that crossed Wade's features. 'I did say I wasn't going,' she went on to remind him, and it struck her how very strange it was that she should be endeavouring to mollify him, just as if he had some authority over her.

His face relaxed, much to her relief; he appeared to be affected by her urgency to appease and, just as if he would set her mind at rest, he forced a smile to his lips.

'I'm glad, Lorna, that you showed such common sense. Brock should have known better than ask you to go alone with him to Brisbane.'

Lorna responded to his smile, her world bright and rosy again.

'I don't think he gave the matter sufficient thought,' she said. 'He might have concluded that I wasn't having much excitement here.'

'You're not, are you?'

She shook her head in agreement, but the smile was still there, in her eyes now as well as hovering on her lips.

'I have so many other things that excitement doesn't matter. In any case,' she added without thinking, 'I've never had much excitement, and what one's never had one never misses.'

He seemed to be considering this, his gaze transferred to the scene outside – the garden with its swaying palms and exotic flowers, the creek beyond, its meandering course clearly defined by the coolibah trees thickly clothing its banks. They too, wound about, into the far distance, becoming lost somewhere in the foothills of the dark mass of the folded ranges, among whose heights the river's source could be located. A fresh breeze sighed into the room from the mountains, imparting a welcome coolness to the air.

'Not much excitement,' murmured Wade to himself, looking at her. 'Your life's been very dull, hasn't it, Lorna?'

Was he asking if she had any regrets? Yes ... oh, but yes! her heart answered. At twenty-one she had been blinded by a sense of duty and compassion; she had made the sacrifice, heartbreaking though it was. And she had hurt the one she loved most; it was only since coming to Bali Creek that it had been fully borne upon her just what she had done, four years ago, when she sent Wade away. He had been passionately in love with her; he knew his love was returned, so all his future must have looked rosy – settled as far as he was concerned. Then, quite suddenly, all his hopes and dreams had been shattered – rendered lifeless by the fact of the accident that had maimed her fiancé, the accident that had been responsible for Lorna's making a decision which Wade could neither understand nor forgive. Sheer anguish swept over her now as she visualized his homecoming ... the pain and frustration and the endless black highway of the future stretching ahead. Had he at that time given one small thought to her own suffering? Perhaps ... but he would find no compassion in his heart for her, since it was her decision and hers alone that had brought such unhappiness to them both.

'For the most part it was dull,' she answered at last, suddenly awake to the fact of his waiting patiently for her reply.

'For the most part? You did have some less dull interludes, then?'

What was he asking her this time?

'After – after my m-marriage, there weren't any less – less ...' Tears came unbidden, choking the rest of the

112

sentence. The moment was overcharged with tension ... with an emotion that seemed to fill the whole room.

'Before your marriage, Lorna?' He was heartless in his persistence, yet she knew instinctively that he was being driven by something beyond his control, some force that had him in its grip – a cruel force that knew no pity; it was a legacy from the primitive, when mercy and compassion were traits as yet unknown. 'Before your marriage you had excitement? You knew what it was to be happy—'

'Stop,' she cried in anguish, 'please! Why are you trying to torture me? I know I made the wrong decision – you have no need to remind me—'

'At the time you insisted it was the right decision!' Blue veins stood out starkly against the bronzed skin of his temples; his eyes were on fire with anger. 'Before your marriage you knew what love was – and yet you tossed it away as easily as if it had been some worthless thing! Tears—' A sneer rolled his underlip. How different he was from the man of a few moments ago when, affected by her urgency to coax him into a more softened mood, he had brought forth the smile that had set her world to rights again 'How easily they come now, but you didn't cry at the time—'

'I couldn't, Wade. I seemed – numbed by the catastrophe; I had no feelings at all for weeks.' Unconsciously she wrung her hands, oblivious of the fact that on releasing the edges of her wrap it had swung open, revealing her scantily-clad body. 'What are you trying to do to me?' she whispered, her eyes bright with tears. 'It's all in the past, and now – now you're engaged to someone else. . . .'

He looked down at her, and swallowed convulsively, as if something painful had lodged in his throat. But

113

pity was absent in his eyes and his mouth was tight.

'Yes,' he said at last, turning from her. 'Yes, it is all in the past – and I am engaged to someone else.' He swung round again and for one brief moment his eyes swept her figure. And then he left the room, and the door closed softly behind him.

CHAPTER SEVEN

IT was only natural that the scene enacted should leave a deep impression on her, and as she stood looking out from her bedroom window half an hour later her nerves were still disordered by the encounter. Why had Wade brought up the past like that? It was not what she would ever have expected, for he was the aloof type, the type whose emotions would be kept firmly reined, whose manner of unruffled calm would never be disturbed. But it had been disturbed; his fury was almost as frightening as that which she had witnessed four years ago – but not quite as frightening, as on that previous occasion he had been fighting for his future, wrathfully commanding her to drop her dogmatic attitude and see clearly just what she was doing with both their lives.

Lorna's mouth quivered at the memory, and she turned, regarding herself in the mirror. Her face was red, her eyes puffed up, and still far too bright even now, as the tears were building up at the backs of her eyes, striving for release. Her glance strayed to the window again; the solemn solitude of the lonely bush suited her mood as well as offering balm to her hurts and she decided to walk.

She had not gone far when she began to wonder if she ought to return, for both her aunt and Wade would be wondering why she hadn't put in an appearance at the tea table. The thought of food was almost nauseating and with a sort of aggressive resistance to the requirements of conformity she increased her pace, filled with the urge to put some distance between herself and the people who were sitting there, waiting, and probably commenting on her lateness.

'I'll please myself what I do!' she said fiercely. 'Why should I always feel compelled to suit my actions to the needs and the convenience of others? I won't! For once I'm free – free to do as I like!' And in this emotional mood of defiance, brought on by frayed nerves and unhappiness and the scene with Wade, she had only one desire – to be alone, quite alone out in the wilderness, where there was no need to talk, to act as if she had nothing on her mind, just for the sake of her aunt; no need to stem the tears, replacing them with inane smiles, no need to force unwanted food down her, just to satisfy the two who would be watching – and questioning if she appeared not to have an appetite. 'No, I won't sit there and do as you both want me to! I don't want to eat, or drink, or join in your chatter! And why should I be forced to laugh when I feel like crying? Why can't I do what *I* want to do!'

Tears came then, and she allowed them to fall, not troubling to seek for a handkerchief. And she walked on and on, into the quietness and the peace. How good it was to be away from people! She saw a flock of galahs flying in the distance and a smile rose spontaneously to her lips. Nature . . . and the creatures that never went out of their way to hurt. Wade had gone out of his way to hurt, bringing up the past like that for no reason at all. He didn't care any more about what happened all that time ago; he was engaged, his future was now neatly set out before him, with a wife there to come home to after a hard day in the bush; and children would come – children with whom he could romp and whose growth and progress over the years would be a joy and satisfaction to him which she herself would never know.

116

With all this, why should he deliberately reap up the past just in order to hurt her? Of course, he had no idea she still cared, Lorna conceded, and so perhaps he hadn't realized just how deeply he could hurt her. Nevertheless, his taunts and accusations and reminders had been profitless and Lorna could not for the life of her see why he had tortured her with them.

The sun was well down when suddenly she looked around to discover she had walked for several miles. She glanced at her watch, and her heart gave a frightened little jerk as she realized she had been walking for almost an hour and a half. Darkness would drop swiftly, and she would then have difficulty in finding her way home. Finding her way. . . . Another sickening little jerk of her heart as the stark truth was borne upon her.

She had no idea which way she had come, no recollection of the directions of the various bush tracks along which she had walked.

'Perhaps,' she faltered, staring all around her, 'I'll be able to see the homestead lights, in a few moments, when they put them on.'

Instinctively she turned and went back along the track on which she now was, but barely a hundred yards farther on was an intersection and on reaching it she stood still, totally confused as to the track she must take. She had walked on blindly, not thinking, nor even caring, where she was going. With the obsession of wanting to be alone she had desired only to put a great distance between her and the homestead, never pausing for a single moment to think about going back.

Taking the track to her right, she walked briskly along it for about a quarter of a mile, then turned and retraced her steps, sure she had made the wrong choice. But, once back at the crossroads, she was as bewildered

117

as ever.

'I think that perhaps I came straight on,' she said, quite audibly. 'Yes, if I carry on along here I might be heading in the right direction.' But another intersection loomed up, and another, and as darkness swept down over the bushlands she knew that she was hopelessly lost. ...

How long had she slept? Lorna sat up in the long grass and peered into the blackness around her. No lights anywhere. What time was it? She had trudged on and on, she remembered, rubbing the sleep out of her eyes, and then, all hope of locating the homestead by its lights having died, she had sat down for a rest. She remembered curling herself up, and resting her head on her arm, and she remembered no more.

The blood-curdling cry of a dingo on the hunt shattered the unearthly silence for a fleeting moment, but then it dropped again, mingling with the inky blackness and creating an unreal nebulous world of infinite space – a void in which no life existed except that of her own. She shivered and sat up, pushing into the far subterranean of her consciousness all thoughts of her aunt and Wade, and the trouble she had caused, and would continue to cause, until she was found.

She tried to probe the blackness, looking for the outline of the mountains, but they were not discernible. It was useless to move, even, let alone make an attempt to find her way back to the homestead, and she sat down again, aware of a parched throat and limbs stiff and aching from the hours spent in a crouched position. A shudder quivered through her as the cry of a dingo was heard again, filtering the void to give the lie to the impression that no other living creature occupied this black wilderness. The deep hush following the dingo's call fell like a smothering blanket and Lorna actually found herself inhaling a little frantically, as if she were afraid of the supply of air being suddenly cut off.

Inevitably the time came when her vision of the reaction to her absence could no longer be suppressed, and with a growing sense of her own culpability she pictured her aunt's anxiety, which would have begun at teatime when after waiting for her niece's appearance she would quite naturally waste no time in deciding to find out the reason why she had not joined Wade and herself for tea. Wade, Lorna surmised, would not be surprised by her absence, taking it for granted that, still affected by the scene he had caused, she was remaining in her room. But when Aunt Bertha discovered she was not in her room, nor anywhere in the house or grounds, Wade would instantly become anxious – not because of any feelings for her personally, but simply because, as his guest, she was under his care, as it were, just as any other guest would have been.

With increasing apprehension Lorna allowed her thoughts to fly on; she saw the whole household being alerted, questions asked to ascertain who had been the last to see her, or whether anyone had noticed her leaving the grounds and if so, at what time.

'Oh, dear. . . .' She felt in one moment of sheer panic that she would prefer to die, out here in the bush, than face Wade's wrath when eventually she was found by some member of the search party he must inevitably send out. 'Whatever made me do it?'

Her thirst was growing and her stomach felt empty, so that she knew an uncomfortable fluttering which was a prelude to the sensation of weakness which hunger invariably produced.

How long would it be before she was found? She felt sure that Wade himself would take part in the search, in which case his business in Yarralinga would have to be postponed. He would be in a white-hot fury with her, and she admitted she deserved it all. Poor Auntie — she would not have gone to bed, but would be waiting through the long hours, her anxiety for her niece's safety increasing with every moment that passed.

'If only I could see my watch!' But it was impossible and, afraid of attracting the attention of some wild bull or pack of marauding dingoes, she slid down into the grass again and sat very still, every moment seeming like an hour — an hour of sheer torture as one moment she was weighed down by guilt at the trouble she was causing and the next being tortured by her thirst, and the empty feeling in the pit of her stomach.

Supposing they didn't find her. ... They would! She strove to reassure herself, but without success. Terror began to pluck at her nerves as imagination raced forward and she saw herself becoming weaker and weaker....

She heard the throb of an engine overhead and managed to rise from her cramped position among the spinifex tussocks. She waved her arms, rather feebly, for it was over twenty-four hours since she had left the homestead and the heat of the sun had robbed her both of body water and of strength. After trudging for hours during the morning she had at last succumbed to the needs of fatigue and had rested under the shade of a small clump of trees, and it was just at that time that she heard the sound of an aeroplane overhead. She had been dozing and by the time she had come to sufficiently to run from her shelter the plane was becoming smaller and smaller as, frantically, she had waved her arms, tears of sheer disappointment and hopelessness flooding her cheeks. For a long while she remained out in the open, but, exhausted and suffering extreme discomfort from sunburn on her arms and legs, she once again sought the shelter of a small copse. And once again fate had chosen this time to let the searcher fly overhead.

'Come back – come *back*!' she had cried, and then sank down where she stood; and she had never moved until the throb of the aeroplane engine was heard for the third time, and now she continued waving, beside herself with terror lest the pilot should miss her even yet again. And at first it did seem that he had missed her, for he was flying away; she cried out despite the knowledge of the futility of her plea,

'Don't go! Look back again – *please* look back!' She watched the dark object against the sky, her body seeming to be detached from her brain, so numbed were her limbs and so dead the feeling in the pit of her stomach, while her brain continued to cry out, but silently, for the pilot to look back.

The plane circled suddenly and feeling returned to her body as her heart gave a great lurch and her nerves went taut with expectancy. She lifted her arms; he had seen her, she realized, and with the impact of sheer relief came a return of that sensation of lost feeling. But this time it affected her mind as well as her body and as the pilot continued to circle around, looking for a place to land, she was conscious of a slow paralysis enveloping her, a paralysis which resulted in total oblivion.

She awoke to a spectacle of white walls and the smell of antiseptic, and realized at once that she was in the small hospital that was situated about half a mile from the school and which she and her aunt had noticed one day when they had been out walking.

'The boss had it built some years ago,' a nurse had said when, on seeing her by the gate, Lorna and her aunt had stopped for a few minutes to put one or two questions to her. 'It isn't used much, though – although we don't want it to be used much, naturally,' she had added with a smile.

Lorna closed her eyes again, aware of burning limbs. Slowly, as with the clearing of a mist dissolving in the sun's first bright rays, her mind became released from the remaining vestiges of insensibility and memory flooded in with all that had happened between the time of her going off alone into the bush to the moment when relief at the knowledge that she was to be rescued had the effect of rendering her unconscious.

What had occurred since then? – and how long had she been here? Turning her head on sensing a movement beside the bed, she looked up into the tired eyes of the Boss of Bali Creek. No sound left her lips even though she opened them to voice an apology for all the trouble she had caused. She had transgressed against the most important rule of the Outback, a rule which had been made known to her by Wade right at the beginning, and which she had completely forgotten in that first hour and a half as she walked unheeding into the bush.

'How are you feeling, Lorna?' Quiet tones and anxious. Lorna gave a surprised start, wondering how his anger came to be suppressed and speculating with some trepidation on whether or not she would feel its brunt once she admitted she was feeling all right. 'You're burned, though,' he said after she had answered him. 'You must be experiencing some pain?'

'Yes,' she nodded, 'I do have a stinging in my legs and arms.' She paused, but he made no comment. 'I'm so sorry, Wade, for all the trouble I've put everyone to.' She said no more, since it struck her that whatever she offered in explanation or excuse must sound ludicrous, bringing down both anger and derision on her head. 'Was it you who found me?' she managed after a while, and he nodded his head.

'Yes—' He stopped and she noted the nerve pulsating in the side of his jaw. 'I'd begun to give up hope. I knew you couldn't be too far away, being on foot, and yet I couldn't spot you.'

'I heard the plane, on two occasions, but each time I was sheltering among the trees I dozed, you see, and by the time I'd caught the sound, and roused myself sufficiently to run from my cover, you were flying away. It was you, in the aeroplane all the time?'

'I had a couple of breaks, driving around in one of the utes while Robert flew the plane.' His face was grim, but still no anger was evidenced in his tones or his manner. Had he been dreadfully anxious about her? But yes, naturally. He would be anxious about anyone who was lost in that wilderness out there; it didn't have any significance, this anxiety she saw. She had been merely a *person* missing, not the girl he had once so dearly loved. 'What made you go off like that, without saying a word to anyone?'

She coloured, wondering what she could say to that, the question she had dreaded from the moment of finding herself lost.

'I had a desire to be alone for a while.' How weak it sounded, and for one impulsive moment she almost blurted out the truth, confessing to being so deeply hurt by the scene which had taken place between them that she had wanted only to get away, to be by herself, in the silence and the peace of the bush where her tears could fall without hindrance, unchecked by the necessity of her having to assume a cheerful front at the tea-table. But as such an admission would be in effect a confession that her love for him was still strong within her she naturally suppressed the words that rose to her lips. 'I really have no excuse,' she ended lamely, fully expecting to see his anger released. But although she did gain the impression of his being angry with her, she also sensed a reluctance on his part to demonstrate his anger at this stage. His next words confirmed the idea.

'You're safe, and that's all that matters at present. You'll remain here for a couple of days—'

'Two days?' she broke in without thinking. She was getting off lightly, for the moment, and she ought not to argue with anything Wade had to say regarding the arrangements that had been made for her.

'Yes, Lorna,' he answered firmly. 'You'll be under observation during that time. This is usual and the doctor has ordered it.'

She nodded meekly then and asked,

'Auntie ... she's been dreadfully worried about me?'

'Naturally,' with the hint of censure entering his voice. 'We've all been dreadfully worried about you.'

Lorna caught her underlip between her teeth.

'I'm sorry—' she began, but Wade instantly interrupted her, a rough edge to his words.

'Never mind. Your aunt's sleeping at present; that's why she isn't here. She sat with you for a short time after I brought you in, but I told her to go to bed.'

'She's – been up all night?'

Wade looked straight into Lorna's eyes.

'We've all been up all night – the whole community here was alerted.' He rose then, turning his head as the doctor came into the ward.

'You're awake. Good!' Dr. Enderson's rugged face was set in stern and admonishing lines. 'What in the name of heaven made you go off like that? Had no one told you that it's definitely against the rules we have here?'

She nodded against the pillow.

'Yes, Wade told me, right at the beginning.' Her voice caught, revealing the tenseness within her, and when the doctor would have spoken again Wade intervened with,

'Let it rest, Howard, for the time being. I'll go now. Lorna's aunt will probably be over later this evening.'

Lorna said, again without thinking,

'You, Wade . . . will you be coming with her?'

An odd glance was Wade's response to this. He would have spoken, but the doctor was before him.

'The Boss requires sleep. He's been searching for you this past twenty-four hours or more.'

Utterly deflated and ashamed, Lorna turned her head away. The next moment she was alone, the two men having left the ward together.

Her aunt came after dinner, having been driven over in the homestead car by Stuart, who although having taken part in the search, had given up in the early afternoon and gone to bed, having been dropping to sleep for hours before then.

'You're all right now, dear?' Aunt Bertha had taken the chair offered by the smiling young nurse and was looking anxiously into her niece's face. 'Wade went to bed immediately on getting back home, but he left me a message saying you were all right. I got it when I woke up.'

Contritely Lorna met her gaze.

'I don't know what to say, Auntie. I'm so sorry for all the anxiety you've been through—'

'Never heed it now, my child,' broke in her aunt hurriedly. 'It's all over, and you're safely back home.'

'You're kind. . . . You must have been out of your mind with worry?' Lorna felt the weight of guilt increase. Would she ever rid herself of it? she wondered. 'I can't think why I did it. I just forgot everything except the need for total isolation—' She pulled herself up, but too much had already been said. Her aunt looked curiously at her and softly put the question,

'You were unhappy over something?'

Lorna hesitated. But her aunt knew her far too well to be taken in by any white lie which her niece might manufacture, and Lorna nodded her head, admitting that unhappiness was the reason for her going off on her own like that. Her aunt naturally inquired as to the cause of this unhappiness, and again admitting that only the truth would be convincing Lorna said,

'Wade had been a little unkind to me. He – he reminded me of the past. . . .'

A strange silence followed. All anxiety fell from the old lady, and in fact she actually smiled to herself . . . a most satisfied smile, thought Lorna with a dawning frown.

'He did? How extraordinary!' Aunt Bertha looked very much as if she did not consider the matter extraordinary at all, but on noting the puzzled look on Lorna's face she added quickly, 'I shouldn't have thought you'd be too adversely affected by it, though, dear, seeing that you're no longer in love with him.' Something subtle in the way that was said, decided

126

Lorna, and once again became puzzled by her aunt's strange behaviour, which had begun almost from the day she and Lorna had arrived at Bali Creek.

'It hurt, all the same. Reaping up the past always does hurt.'

'Perhaps – yes,' agreed her aunt, nodding her head, 'I expect it does hurt. Er – what exactly did he say, dear?'

It suddenly struck Lorna that her aunt's lack of interest in the ordeal she had suffered, out there alone in the bush all night, amounted almost to callousness. She appeared to be far more interested in what Wade had said, for she was waiting with an expression on her face that could only be described as eagerness.

'He reminded me of the decision I had made – reminded me that it was the wrong decision. He – he seemed resentful still, even though he's now engaged to someone else.'

'Resentful still. . . .' half to herself as Aunt Bertha dwelt on what Lorna had said. She looked at her and added, 'Didn't it strike you as strange that he should seem resentful?'

'He was remembering an old injury. Naturally he'd be resentful – for what he had suffered in the past.'

A strange smile hovered on her aunt's lips on her hearing this. But all she said was.

'I expect you're right, dear. One would be resentful on recalling old hurts.' And then, abruptly veering on to another line of the conversation, 'Wade was here when you regained consciousness. What was his attitude? I mean, was he furious with you?'

'No, not at all. I couldn't understand it. He must have been angry – very, because of all the upset, and his having to postpone his visit to Yarralinga. But he didn't show his anger in any way. On the contrary, he was – was – sort of gentle. ...' Her eyes took on a pensive expression; she forgot her aunt's presence for the moment as she recaptured the vision of Wade, that nerve pulsating in the side of his jaw, saying he had begun to give up hope. Yes, right from the moment she had opened her eyes to see him standing there, by the bed, she had sensed a gentleness about him ... a gentleness which had been so very familiar in those far-off days when she was the only girl in his life, the girl who, he said so confidently, was to become the fourth bride of Bali Creek.

Lorna's eyes glistened at the memory and she turned her head so that her aunt would not see.

'He was gentle, was he?' Aunt Bertha was saying, again half to herself. She also was lost in thought, but what occupied her was obviously much more pleasing than that which brought tears so close to her niece's eyes, for her lips were curved in a smile of undiluted satisfaction.

CHAPTER EIGHT

AMONG the visitors Lorna received during her first full day in hospital were one or two of the stockmen's wives whom she and her aunt had got to know while out on their daily strolls. These brought in fruit and flowers, and books for Lorna to browse through when she was alone. Wade came before lunch, bringing her aunt with him, but when he came later, during the afternoon, he was alone. Aunt Bertha was resting, he told Lorna, but she would be over about six o'clock.

'I expect she's very tired.' Lorna spoke dejectedly, because of her deep sense of guilt and because on his earlier visit Wade had been brusque with her and she felt that very soon now she would have to face his angry questions as to why she had disobeyed his order not to go off into the bush alone. Tomorrow evening she was to be taken to the homestead and then, she surmised, the questions and subsequent admonishment could be expected. 'I suppose *everyone's* very tired.'

Wade stood by the bed, looking down into her face. Her lovely hair fell like a golden halo on to the pillow, her big violet eyes were clouded and her lip quivered. 'I feel so blameworthy— Wade, I want to go home – back to England!' How that came to escape she would never know. She hadn't meant to say anything of the kind; her sudden desire to leave Bali Creek and the man whose presence evoked such a host of memories had found outlet in words which she had not had time to suppress.

'You want to leave here?'

Lorna nodded; she was turned away from his gaze

129

now and the appearance of little grey lines by the sides of his mouth escaped her entirely.

'Yes, Wade, I do want to leave.' There was no sense in trying to retract, not with her desire having been so spontaneously voiced. 'I've enjoyed being here, and I do thank you for having Auntie and me, but I feel we should be thinking of going very soon.'

A silence followed, profound and long.

'Have you talked with your aunt about this?' he inquired at length and, when she shook her head, 'She's very happy here, Lorna. I don't think you should insist on leaving until she herself is ready to go. After all, it might be the last holiday of this sort that she will have. I gather she isn't too well off in the ordinary way, and to curtail the holiday wouldn't be at all kind.'

She turned then, to examine his face. For it did seem that he genuinely wanted them to remain at Bali Creek for some time yet. It was hard for Lorna to believe he had said, on their arrival, that she, Lorna, was not welcome at Bali Creek. That Wade had changed his attitude since then was evident, but what had caused the change was very far from evident.

'I suppose you're right,' conceded Lorna, but with a deep sigh accompanying the words. 'Perhaps I ought not to tell her how I feel.'

'You gave me to believe you liked being here?' Wade drew up a chair and sat down. His attire was rather more formal than his usual tight trousers and open-necked shirt. He wore a dark grey linen jacket and a tie; his shirt was snowy white against his throat. 'Why have you suddenly changed your mind?'

She shrugged a little helplessly.

'I expect it must be owing to the way I'm feeling at present. It was so wrong of me to go off like that. I feel

130

I've disgraced myself irreparably.'

He smiled then, much to her surprise.

'Can it be that you're afraid of what I might say to you, later, when you're fully recovered?' Wade leant back in his chair, his gaze taking in every lovely aspect of her features. She said, lowering her lashes,

'You're obviously very observant, Wade.'

'It isn't difficult to read you, Lorna.'

Her voice reflected her surprise as she said,

'I can't think why you're not angry already.'

'I was at first — exceedingly angry. Had you been found that first night I'd have let you have it, strong and heavy. But you weren't found, and as the hours passed and dawn came, and still you were missing—' He broke off and remained silent for a space, as if speech had become difficult. 'We all began to be seriously worried, and all that mattered from then on was that you would be found, because as time went on we knew that you'd be growing weaker, and of course you'd become unable to move about. Once you were immobile — lying among the tall grasses, it would be a miracle if you were found.'

Lorna said nothing, but just looked at him, and after a moment he added, 'Don't worry yourself unnecessarily, Lorna, I'm not going to lecture you over this. You told your aunt that it was the need for total isolation that had caused you to go out walking as you did—' His grey eyes looked steadfastly into hers. 'I think I understand, Lorna, and because I understand, I'm not intending to cause you any more distress over this business.' And he sought her hand, as it lay on the coverlet, enclosing it in his own, and she felt its warmth and its strength, and its infinite assurance that his promise would be kept. He understood, he had said. He knew, then, that he had hurt her by his unnecessary

131

bringing up of the past, and he was accepting her hurt as an excuse for her conduct in disregarding his order not to stray too far from the homestead. Lorna's heart lightened; she offered him a smile and he responded. 'Do you still want to go home?' he asked gently, and she replied, a shy edge to her voice,

'Not now, Wade. Thank you for not being cross with me; I know I deserve that you should be.'

'And so you were worrying yourself sick?' A crooked smile took the place of the other. 'Am I so formidable to you, Lorna?'

'Not when you're like this.' So strange it was, to be talking together in so intimate a way. Wade's reserve had dissolved completely; he was looking at her with kindness in his eyes; his hand on hers was a gentle caress. He had become accessible all at once and she recalled her hope that he would forgive her before she left his home, left for ever. ... A shadow of pain crossed her face and her mouth trembled. He said with sudden concern,

'What's wrong? You're not feeling ill, are you?'

She shook her head, unwilling to cause him anxiety.

'No, I'm not feeling ill.' And she smiled at him, half turning her head. The sunlight caught her hair, imparting lavish gold to add to its beauty; the light also touched her eyes, enhancing their colour. It accentuated the contours of her face, brought out more plainly the blue veins visible beneath the transparency of the flawless skin over her temples. Wade swallowed thickly, and dragged his gaze from the enchanting picture she made.

'I must go,' he said with startling abruptness as he rose to his feet. 'As I've said, your aunt will be over to spend an hour with you before dinner.'

132

Lorna looked up at him. How handsome he was! And distinguished, with his tall leanness and his straight square shoulders, and the noble way he held his head.

'Thank you for coming,' she said simply. 'It's kind of you, Wade, when you have so many other things to do.'

For a long moment he remained by the bed, staring down into her face, as if reluctant now to leave.

'I'll be over again tomorrow morning,' he promised, smiling. 'And tomorrow evening you'll be coming back with me.'

'I'll be glad to be home again—' She cut off swiftly, having spoken impulsively, without thinking, and the colour rose to her cheeks. Her long dark lashes came down to hide her expression from his deep and intense scrutiny. He continued to watch her, silently. It was a profound moment, hushed and still. It was as if he were dwelling on her words and suddenly she knew that, like her, he was hearing himself say, 'You'll be the fourth bride of Bali Creek . . . and the best loved.'

At length she managed to look up; his eyes brooded, one hand was clenched. He bade her a curt good-bye and left the room.

The doctor came a short while later, expressed his satisfaction and went away again. Lorna was reading a book when the young nurse appeared, to announce another visitor.

'Brock!' Lorna greeted him enthusiastically, lowering her book on to the bed cover. 'How very nice of you to come and see me. Were you doing some business with Wade?' she asked, sending him an interrogating glance.

He came forward into the room and took possession of the chair by the bed.

133

'No, I came over especially to see you.'

'All that way?' She stared unbelievingly. 'You drove here just to see me?'

He leant back in his chair, his eyes roving her face and the pretty bedjacket she wore.

'Why so surprised? If you remember, I did say I'd come over yesterday, but Wade then mentioned that you were all going to town.' He paused, saw that Lorna was embarrassed by what he had said and, with a small sigh, he changed the subject, asking how she managed to get herself lost. 'Wade gave you ample warning, surely? We always do warn visitors who might be ignorant of the hazards which the bush presents.'

'He did warn me, yes. But I forgot about his warning—'

'You forgot!' he echoed. 'How in the name of Lucifer could you forget?'

She shook her head.

'It's hard to explain, Brock. Please don't question me.' She spoke with a certain finality, but gave him time to speak. He refrained and she went on, 'How did you know about my getting lost? Did Wade contact you over the air?'

'He asked for our help.'

'He asked for your help?' A hand stole to Lorna's cheek as imagination flowed unhindered. 'You mean, all your father's stockmen were out searching, as well as Wade's?'

'Wade didn't alert Father until yesterday morning. By that time he decided he required every single man he could get hold of— It seems that, at first, he had no doubts at all about finding you long before dawn, because he estimated that you couldn't have gone far. However, by dawn he decided to ask for our men, and these were sent, naturally.'

'All of them?'

'Most of them.'

'How awful of me to cause all that trouble!' Guilt pressed down again. 'How – how did they come?'

'How did they travel, you mean? By cars. Every vehicle was brought into operation – station wagons, the ute and the homestead car. Some of the men have cars or land-rovers. ...' Mercifully he stopped on noting the flood of colour that gave evidence of her acute discomfiture. 'Don't worry too much about it, Lorna. You're not the first person who's been lost out there.'

'But I ought to have thought about all the trouble and inconvenience I would cause— Oh, I shall never be able to forget it – never!'

'Certainly you will. It's all over and done with.' He paused a moment. 'How are you feeling?'

'There's nothing wrong with me, except that I'm burned, of course.'

He nodded understandingly.

'Sunburn can be hell. But the thirst – that must have been hell too?'

She shuddered at the memory, although her mind was still occupied with the trouble she had caused to everyone.

'It was,' she answered briefly, and Brock changed the subject.

'I had to come and see you, Lorna. Wade doesn't know I'm here, but I'll call at the homestead before I leave, of course.' Something in his tone brought a return of her former embarrassment. She hoped Brock was not going to complicate the remainder of her stay at Bali Creek.

'It was kind of you,' she murmured, and then, before he could speak. 'Your people – were they annoyed at having to send their men off to look for me?' She was thinking about Olga, and wondering if, when they next met, the girl would come out with some derisive comments about those people who fail to treat the terrain with due respect.

'Annoyed? – certainly not. It isn't the first time we've been called out. Last year a party of tourists were lost. They'd left their car after it broke down and one of our men saw it as he was going into Yarralinga. He turned back, naturally, and both our men and Wade's went off to find them. Stupid lot! They must have been told that the best chance of survival is to stay with your vehicle. Had they done that they'd scarcely have suffered at all. As it was, it took us two full days to find them, and as they'd been walking round in circles before that, they were in a pretty bad way. They were brought to the hospital here and had to stay for about four days, I think it was.'

'People don't realize the dangers. I suppose that if your car breaks down you naturally begin looking for water – once you've used up your reserve, that is.'

Brock nodded.

'That's what happened in this case. They thought they might find a stream— A stream out here, and in the Dry! I ask you!' Brock turned as the nurse entered.

'Are you having tea with Lorna, Mr. Norville?'

'Just a drink, please.' He was not one for afternoon tea, he went on to tell Lorna when the nurse had gone. 'I'd rather wait for my dinner, and make a feast of it.'

He stayed for another half-hour, then left.

'I'll see you at Wade's barbecue,' he said, turning at the door.

Lorna smiled and nodded, then her eyes lit up. Aunt Bertha was there in the doorway, beaming at Brock,

136

who had stepped aside to allow her to pass in front of him.

'Brock . . . well, how thoughtful of you to come and see Lorna. Does Wade know you're here?' The sudden change from greeting to inquiry was so markedly abrupt as to bring a tiny gasp to Lorna's lips. Brock had driven over a hundred miles in the heat of the day and all that interested her aunt was whether or not Wade knew of his presence at the hospital.

'Not yet—'

'You must call at the homestead, then.'

Brock looked oddly at her, then exchanged glances with Lorna.

'I was about to say I intended going over there – now.'

Aunt Bertha went a trifle red.

'Sorry I interrupted,' she muttered, coming towards the bed. 'I should have known you would be calling on Wade before you left.'

'You appear to be most anxious for me to call upon him, Mrs. Gerrard.' Brock sounded as though he could not help uttering these words. He was puzzled by the urgency of the interruption, as was Lorna.

Aunt Bertha shrugged with well-feigned indifference.

'Me – anxious? But why should I be anxious for you to call on Wade? No – I merely spoke unthinkingly, as one does, you know, when one's mind is on other things.'

Lorna said, watching her aunt's face closely,

'What things are on your mind?'

'Why, you, of course! I can't stop thinking of the dreadful ordeal you went through. It fairly makes me tremble!'

Lorna eyed her suspiciously, recalling how casually

137

her aunt had passed off the matter of the twenty-four hours spent in the bush. However, she made no comment, merely bidding Brock good-bye as he lifted a hand before leaving the room.

'Sit down, Auntie. How have you come? Did Stuart bring you again?'

'Yes. Isn't it kind of him? Of course, it wouldn't have done me any harm to walk, but Wade wouldn't hear of it. He's so thoughtful, that young man. He said I might be all right walking here, but would I feel like walking back. No, he said – in that firm way he has – I would be far too tired, so he would have someone drive me here. And now, dear, how are you feeling? You look very well, I must say – and comfortable, sitting there against the pillows.'

'I'm exceedingly comfortable. And I feel no after-effects; even the burns are less painful than they were earlier this morning.'

Her aunt seemed miles away. After having asked the question she now appeared to have no interest whatsoever in her niece's reply.

'I wonder what Wade will think – Brock coming all this way just to see you.' She spoke softly, to herself, and Lorna scarcely caught the gist of what she said. 'I myself never even thought he'd go as far as that.'

Lorna shook her head, a little exasperated by her lack of ability to understand her aunt these days. Best leave her alone, she decided. Let her ramble on if she so wished.

However, Aunt Bertha immediately went on to other things, chatting casually until it was time to leave.

'Good night, dear.' She bent and kissed Lorna's cheek. 'I'm so glad you haven't suffered as a result of your dreadful experience,' she added, but Lorna felt convinced it was said as an afterthought.

Why should she be so interested in Wade's reaction to Brock's visit? Lorna wondered with a frown, her eyes fixed on the closed door through which her aunt had just departed. It was most unlikely that Wade would show any reaction at all. But that was where Lorna was wrong. No sooner had he arrived at the hospital the following morning than he said shortly, and with a grim expression in his eyes,

'Brock seems inordinately interested in you. You should be feeling honoured that he would come all this way merely to spend an hour or so with you.'

Lorna looked swiftly at him. She was sitting up against the pillows, looking enchantingly pretty, having just brushed her hair until it shone, and put on a rose quilted bedjacket which her aunt had brought in on her first visit.

'I was surprised myself,' she admitted, her gaze frank, and slightly puzzled because of the tightness of Wade's mouth and that grim expression in his eyes. 'If he was anxious about me he could have inquired over the air as to how I was.'

'He was certainly anxious,' tersely as Wade sat down on the chair. 'There's no doubt about that.'

Lorna's puzzlement grew.

'Are you vexed at his coming?' she asked a little nervously.

His head came up; he appeared arrogant all at once.

'Vexed? Why should I be vexed?'

Lorna spread her hands.

'There's no reason ... but you don't seem too pleased.' Her lip quivered and he frowned suddenly on noting it. He said more gently,

'I'm not displeased, if that's what you mean. It was

139

merely that Brock's visit surprised me. He didn't even let me know he was coming.' Lorna said nothing and after a small pause Wade went on, watching her closely, 'Brock usually gets no further than flirting.'

'Brock has never flirted with me,' she returned indignantly, 'nor has he got any further!'

'I take your word for the first statement, but not the second. You might not yet have grasped the fact, but Brock is definitely interested in you.' The acceptance of this brought a momentary frown to Wade's forehead, but then his face became an angular mask – uncommunicative, unreadable.

'Then Brock wastes his time,' Lorna said quietly. 'For *I* am certainly not interested in *him*.'

Wade said,

'You don't find him attractive?'

'Undoubtedly he's attractive. How could it be otherwise? He has so much – looks, physique, charm of manner. One day some girl is going to fall head over heels in love with him.'

Faintly Wade smiled, but without humour. He was distant, withdrawn into himself and his thoughts. His eyes brooded, as if these thoughts were far from pleasant.

'So you do find him attractive?'

She shook her head, bewildered by his manner. Were it not for the fact of his being engaged to Olga she could almost have sensed jealousy smouldering beneath the smooth and even timbre of his voice.

'I said he was attractive. You either misunderstood my words or you twisted them.' She spoke a little haltingly, her one urgent desire being to coax him to a gentle mood, a mood that would lighten her heart and provide another happy memory to add to her store.

'I'm sorry,' was his unexpected response. 'I take it

140

that although you admit to his being a charmer, in every way, he hasn't the ability to charm you?'

She paused a moment, watching as he unconsciously teetered back on his chair, his eyes narrowed from habit, the habit of shielding them from the sun.

'I'm not in the mood to be charmed, Wade. Auntie and I came here for a holiday, and as we shall be leaving soon it would be stupid of me to become involved with Brock.'

Wade nodded, but her words about Brock were passed over as he said,

'I don't think you'll be leaving soon. Your aunt is very contentedly settled in.'

She looked at him in surprise.

'Don't you mind how long we stay?'

'We like having visitors; it makes a pleasant change from our own company.'

'Auntie has a house, and a garden.'

'Who is looking after them for her?'

'Two neighbours, but we can't stay away indefinitely.'

His grey eyes searched her face.

'Tell me, what will you do once you're home again?'

'I shall go back to my job – if it's been kept open for me, which I hope it has.'

'And at the week-ends?'

'I do a few chores, or a little baking. Mainly, I spend my time in the garden – in the spring and summer, that is. Auntie isn't too strong really, and gardening's too heavy for her.' Her candid gaze was directed towards his; the sun streaming through the window was thin as yet and not very flattering as it accentuated her pallor. But Wade's eyes seemed, strangely, to be flickering with admiration. Lorna's colour rose, relieving the pallor instantly, and a half-smile fluttered to her lips so that they trembled a little before straightening out again. A profound silence ensued, while his cool gaze never wavered from her face. At length he shook his head.

'You haven't much variety—' He broke off, half-frowning as he glanced away. She knew instinctively that he was angry with himself for the slip which revealed thoughts he had meant to keep to himself. She hadn't much variety in her life.... Was he pitying her? Every nerve in her body rebelled as the certainty of this was borne in upon her. Pity! She looked back, recalling one incident after another when he had acted in a way that could be stamped as pity. And now ... his face was drawn, his brow creased in a frown. He was thinking about her life, glimpsing its dullness, picturing the monotony ... and perhaps in addition to the pity he felt for her was the thought that she had only herself to blame, since her life could have been so very different had she made a decision which was prompted by the dictates of heart rather than conscience. A chill swept over her and automatically she clutched the covers and pulled them up against her chest. Her pallor had returned; the stare she gave him was cool and indignant and a puzzled line appeared between his eyes at this sudden change in her expression.

'My life's quite full,' she asserted stiffly. 'There's no excitement, as I admitted before, but there's contentment. I'm – I'm perfectly satisfied with my lot.'

Clearly taken aback by the manner in which this was delivered, he came forward in his chair – so close he came, his jaw taut and his eyes glinting as if anger lurked, that he seemed more than a little frightening. And yet ... how she loved him! It was sheer agony no to put forth a hand silently inviting him to take it, as he

142

had so willingly taken it at every opportunity in those days when his love for her was so passionate and strong. It was agony not to lean forward, a smile quivering on her lips, and rest her head on his shoulder, possessively, because it was *her* shoulder and she had every right to be there. A heaviness collected behind her eyes and her heart felt dead, because instead of these things she yearned so fervently to do she had to assume a cool unemotional front, had to hold her head high just to demonstrate that pride was in the ascendancy. Wade rose abruptly, as if aware his presence was no longer desired. In words as stiffly voiced as her own he bade her good-bye and left her, left her biting hard on her lip and swallowing convulsively. Pity. It was too humiliating, too unbearable. An attitude of total indifference on Wade's part would have been preferable.

CHAPTER NINE

IT was the evening before the barbecue and as usual the after-dinner coffee was served on the verandah. Stuart and Robert and the two students were conversing a little apart from Wade and Aunt Bertha, who were also immersed in conversation; and Lorna, having subsided comfortably into the rattan chair, was left to her own thoughts. Still smarting under the knowledge that without any doubt at all she was the object of Wade's pity, she had, immediately on returning from the hospital, adopted an air of cool detachment which was in effect a protective cloak, worn whenever she found herself in Wade's company. And as inevitably his own pride put a check on any advances on his part the relationship between the two deteriorated without any obvious reason, and less than twenty-four hours after he had brought her from the hospital they had somehow managed to reach the stage where they were speaking to one another only when it was absolutely necessary. Puzzled, Aunt Bertha had tackled Lorna, who had not hesitated to tell her the truth.

'Wade pities me! And I'm not willing to be pitied. If I remain cool with him he'll soon begin to see that I'm not begging for his kindness, or compassion. I've suspected him of pitying me, and had already begun to resent it. When he visited me at the hospital he said something which strengthened my previous idea, and so I've decided to treat him with very marked coolness for the rest of our stay here. I'm sorry, Auntie, to have to do this, but I have my pride, and I hope you will try to understand just how I'm feeling. A girl who's once had a man's love doesn't want to find herself left with his pity.'

Aunt Bertha's dismay on hearing this was out of all proportion.

'Pity— Oh, no, Lorna dear, you're quite wrong! I'm sure you're wrong!' She looked almost ready to cry, thought Lorna with a frown, and was instantly sorry she had not practised a little more tact. Obviously her aunt was now feeling guilty, regretting bringing Lorna here – to be pitied by Wade instead of regaining his love. However, it was now too late to retract and Lorna reluctantly assured her aunt that what she said was quite true.

'He's been kind – and even gentle, you must have noticed. And he never uttered a word of censure over my getting lost. I've seen his pity displayed several times lately, especially in his expression. I know I'm right, Auntie.'

'Well. . . .' A deep sigh and then Aunt Bertha said something to herself, something which sounded like, 'I never took this aspect into consideration,' but Lorna could not be sure, and in any case, her aunt cut the sentence off sharply, as if afraid her niece should hear what in effect were merely her own private thoughts, uttered involuntarily. Lifting her eyes to Lorna's puzzled face, she was for a fleeting moment ill at ease, but swiftly recovered, saying with a flip of her hand, 'I wouldn't have said myself that I noticed anything resembling pity in his manner towards you, Lorna dear. But in any case, why should you take it so to heart? He's only being compassionate, which is natural.'

'You consider I should be deriving a sort of bitter comfort from his pity?' Lorna was angry as a result of her aunt's attitude. Her aunt failed utterly to under-

145

stand what it felt like to receive pity in place of a love that was lost forever. Of course, she had told her aunt emphatically that she no longer cared for Wade, so perhaps there was some excuse for the way she spoke. Her aunt had let the matter drop, but now, as she chatted with Wade, she would glance occasionally at Lorna, as if the memory of her niece's assertion were running through her mind. These glances began to vex Lorna, who secretly admitted that her nerves were more than a little on edge, the result of the strained atmosphere existing between Wade and herself.

'I think I'll go to bed,' she said at length, her glance embracing the entire company. 'If you'll excuse me . . .?'

Wade cast her a glance as she rose and made a move to enter the house.

'You're feeling tired?' The glance swept her arms, red and sore from the burns received from the merciless sun. Lorna nodded her head.

'Yes, Wade, I do feel rather tired.'

She wondered if he frowned, or whether she imagined it. Whatever his emotions compassion rose well above the rest; this much she knew. Well, he could keep his compassion! Her chin lifted and her eyes stared straightly into his. Her mouth was set in an arrogant line; she saw his eyes narrow, and the hand resting on the arm of his chair suddenly closed.

'Then go to bed by all means. I hope you'll feel better in the morning,' and he turned to say something to her aunt. Lorna knew she had been snubbed and even though she could not deny she had asked for the snub, her lip trembled as a wave of self-pity swept over her.

She did not go to her room, but stole out into the silence of the garden, keeping to the back, out of sight

146

of the people on the verandah. A small secluded arbour invited and she sat down on the stone seat. Voices drifted to her across the distance, voices of some of Wade's stockmen, sitting outside one of the bungalows; something closer to made a scurrying sound, then actually ran over Lorna's feet. Probably a small marsupial, she thought, out on a nocturnal hunt for food. She sat very still, looking around, hoping to see a pair of black eyes, like shiny beads, popping out of the creature's head. But it had gone, leaving no trace. She leant back, and stared into the heavens, where the Southern Cross spangled the sky, a dramatic mosaic against a backcloth of deepest purple. Another sound . . . the soft but firm footfall she could not possibly mistake. She shrank back even while aware she had not escaped detection.

'I thought you said you were going to bed.' Sharp the tone, and faintly accusing. 'You merely wanted to be alone again, is that it?'

She straightened up on her seat, put out somewhat by the fact of his having observed her move to hide herself from his view. He stood in the entrance to the bower, tall and straight in the starlight, one hand in his pocket, the other resting against a support of the trellis. Behind him the lower outlines of the mountains could be discerned, darkly etched against the sky, while their summits were lost in a tapestry of low-lying woolpacks.

'I did want to be alone, yes.' She spoke softly, affected by his presence and wondering at the same time what had brought him out into the garden, away from his guests. 'It — it's fresh out here, and it was rather early to go to bed.'

'You discovered that only after you'd left us, apparently?'

147

She swallowed, endeavouring to ease the dry ache that had settled in her throat.

'Discovered that it was too early to go to bed? Yes, I suppose I did realize this only after I'd left you all.'

His face became grim. He took a couple of steps into the arbour, but made no attempt to take possession of the vacant place beside her.

'You appear to be extraordinarily fond of your own company,' he remarked, an edge to his voice that cut her deeply.

She found herself wishing she could confide in him, speak intimately with him, telling him of her life with her husband, and how she would have to go off on her own, walking the lanes in order to get away from the incessant stream of grumbles and complaints, the gross ingratitude, but of course she refrained. In the first place she would immediately succeed in increasing the pity which Wade already felt for her, and secondly, she could ever bring herself to tell anyone the whole of what she had been through during her three and a half years of marriage, for she knew in her heart that it was her husband's inactivity, his imprisonment in a wheelchair, that had soured him and bred such discontent that he was out of humour for the greater part of his time, finding fault instead of extending a word of praise, snapping at her when he ought to have been making her lot easier by a smile of encouragement.

'Sometimes it's pleasant to have one's own company,' she offered at last, noting that Wade was expecting some response to his remark.

'What do you think about when you're on your own like this?' The coolness was still there, but not nearly so pronounced as it had been during the past day or so. She could foresee its dissolving altogether and this she did not want, since it would mean a return to the situation she wished to avoid – the situation where she was being pitied by Wade. And yet, paradoxically, she yearned for his kindness, for the gentle note to enter his voice and the matching smile to rise to his lips.

She recalled that moment of meeting again after the long separation; she had not changed, she was soon to discover. She could have gone to him, gladly, and allowed herself to be enfolded in his strong possessive embrace, could have lifted her face for his kiss, undisguised love in her eyes. But a reunion was not to be, not then or at any other time. All Auntie's hopes – and indeed Lorna's own – had been in vain. They had come out to Australia only to find that Wade was engaged to someone else.

'All sorts of things,' she answered evasively as Wade stirred with slight impatience at yet another long pause before receiving a response from her. 'But mainly,' she added, anticipating another question, 'I just relax my mind – one can, out here, where it's so peaceful and quiet, and so close to nature.'

'You're very attached to this place, aren't you, Lorna?' Soft the words, and a warning tingle caused a touch of pride to transform her features, hardening them slightly.

'I like it,' she admitted with a frankness she could not withhold. 'It's frightening country, as I once told you, but it has a beauty and attraction that surely must be unique.' She was polite in manner, casual in speech. There was neither enthusiasm nor insincerity in her voice. She glanced up as she spoke, forgetting Wade for one brief moment as she absorbed the spectacle of ethereal grandeur displayed in the tropical sky. The moon had emerged from the drifting clouds, adding its pure silver radiance to that emitted by the stars; the Milky Way travelled on into infinity, a never-ending string of

149

frost-flecked pearls. The wide rangelands slept beneath this tapestry of light and the only sound to stir the air was the whisper of casuarina trees over by the dry creek bed.

Wade came a step nearer and she lifted her eyes towards his face. His lips moved in some strange unfathomable way, but no sound reached her across the distance still separating them. A tense moment; there had been others, since the day of her coming to Bali Creek . . . but none quite so tense as this. Why had he come? He could have passed on and she would have assumed he had not noticed her. He must have known this – but he stopped, and spoke . . . and remained.

'Despite this desire for solitude, would you mind very much if I sat down?'

She gave a slight start, because of his tone and manner and the fact that he seemed almost to be pleading with her to agree to his request. Pleading? What an absurd notion! Lorna dismissed it instantly, wondering how it could possibly have entered her mind in the first place.

'It's your arbour,' she said, but gently, driven by some uncontrollable force to drop her proud demeanour and appear more natural. She supposed it was weakness that made her yearn for a small interlude of friendliness to take place between them – before they both, in the colder light of day, reverted to the cool formality which had characterized their relationship since the moment when she had guessed that the kindness shown to her was conceived by pity. 'Of course you can sit down.'

'Thank you.' He occupied the space next to her and stared broodingly towards the mountains; the hush that fell between him and Lorna was no ordinary silence, it accentuated the tenseness; it was alive, vital.

It occupied all their thoughts and each hoped the other would soon break it. It was broken by the shrill blood-curdling cry of a dingo, far away over the inexhaustible bushlands. Involuntarily Lorna made a small move towards her companion, a shudder passing through her.

'Something is soon going to be killed,' she whispered, and now the bush was harsh, merciless, cruel as the great thermal convulsion that brought it into being untold eons of time ago.

'The survival of the fittest,' he returned softly. 'One thing must kill another in order to keep life going.' Was he thinking of the great numbers of cattle he sent away? she wondered, surmising that to him — and in fact to all cattle men — the rearing of livestock for slaughter was wholly a business undertaking, with never a thought to the fact that the poor animals were helpless to do anything about the doom that awaited them in the abattoirs of Katherine and Darwin. She voiced her thoughts, not meaning to, but the words slipped out before she could check them. Wade's face was a study; he said at length,

'Necessity again, Lorna. But at least our animals are happy right up till the time they're sent away, on the cattle-truck trains. It isn't like factory farming where the animals have to be reared and fattened indoors.'

She smiled then and shook her head.

'I know. It was just the thought. I don't like to think of anything being killed.'

'No ... I seem to remember. ...' His voice trailed away, but she knew at once what switch of memory had been responsible for the utterance of those softly-spoken words.

'My little dog got better,' she told him, and he turned and stared into her face.

151

'It didn't have to be put to sleep after all?'

Lorna shook her head.

'The vet operated, and Frisky was as right as rain for another three years. She died peacefully in her sleep – of old age.'

'Well! And so all those tears were shed for nothing?'

She gave a quick self-conscious laugh.

'I went through agony!'

'I remember. It was just three days before—' Abruptly he broke off, but something quite beyond her control made her finish the sentence for him.

'—before we said good-bye. Yes. Wade, I remember it so well. I wept and wept, and in the end you were beginning to get out of patience with me—'

'No, Lorna – I wasn't! I was only troubled that you would make yourself ill. . . .' Again his voice cut, but not so abruptly this time. Something moved in his throat and Lorna wished fervently that the conversation had not followed these painful lines. Wade was deeply affected by memories and so was she.

'Let's change the subject, Wade,' she suggested, and he nodded and turned his head away, staring in front of him for a long moment before saying,

'I half promised I'd take you into Alice. Your aunt's very taken with the idea, so we must do something about it.'

'That's kind of you, Wade.' The situation had eased considerably; Wade's manner had reverted to that of polite host, Lorna's to that of a guest, any ordinary guest. 'Shall we stay a short while, as you said?'

'Of course; you and your aunt will want to see some of the sights.' Faintly he smiled. 'Ayers Rock is a must. No tourist leaves the Alice without having taken a trip over to it.'

Lorna made some reply, and for another quarter of an hour or so they chatted on, saying nothing in particular and yet both secretly loath to put an end to the conversation and return to the homestead, Wade to join the others and Lorna to go to her bedroom.

She cast Wade many a sidelong glance, noted the tenseness of his lean dark features, the nerve pulsating now and then in the side of his jaw. What were his thoughts? she wondered during one rather long lull in the conversation. She had a feeling that the past was vividly with him and that, for the moment, Olga was completely forgotten. There was nothing strange in this, she supposed. Here they were, in this lonely and intimate setting, their nearness to each other deeply felt, she was sure, by Wade as much as by herself; and in such a situation even his fiancée had no place. He stirred and turned his head, set his mouth firmly and turned from her again. What had he been about to say? Whatever it was he had swiftly changed his mind, checking the words she was now destined never to hear. But he spoke presently, and for a few minutes casual conversation was resumed.

Another lull, with silence over the purple landscape — but for the whispering casuarina trees over by the river.

'Perhaps we should be making a move.' Wade's voice cut into the deep hush of the night, its slow Australian drawl carrying something quite unfathomable. He stood up; a gentle breeze blew in suddenly from the mountains, tousling his hair, attractively. Profoundly disturbed, Lorna closed her eyes to his charm, his magnetism. But her heart was beating over-rate and against her will it pleaded, 'Stay a little longer, Wade ... please stay.'

What madness was this? In an attempt to shake it off

she rose abruptly to her feet, but in the swiftness of her movement she twisted her ankle and before she could steady herself Wade had caught her to him. She made a small, half-hearted attempt to draw back, but his hold on her arms tightened.

'Relax,' he ordered as her body stiffened. Obediently she slackened the taut muscles and the next moment she was having her head drawn back as Wade took her hair in his hand and tugged gently at it. His lips were gentle at first, pressing against her eager mouth, and then her cheek and down to her throat. 'So you do love me still, despite the way you've treated me lately.' A statement, followed by another kiss, and another, each growing in ardency until at length Lorna was breathless, her protesting hand against his chest.

'Wade ... please!' she murmured when eventually his hold slackened.

'Please what?' he inquired with a sort of teasing amusement. 'Are you asking for more?'

A wave of colour flooded her cheeks.

'Certainly not!' she retorted, trying to sound indignant. 'I – I was asking you to let me go.'

A raising of his brows, and a quirk of humour in his eyes.

'You yourself are not making much effort to escape, my dear,' he reminded her lightly. 'Are you sure you really want me to let you go?'

It was the last thing she wanted. She said unsteadily,

'Of course I'm sure—'

'Liar!' and she was caught to him again and his lips found hers; they were eager and responding, her arms about him clung tightly and her lovely face was aglow with happiness. Somewhere in the far recesses of her mind was a picture of a girl called Olga, but it *was* only

154

a picture. The girl wasn't of any importance whatsoever; Wade had never really loved her; it was she, Lorna, whom he loved – whom he had never ceased to love; Lorna knew this instinctively, knew by the way he kissed her and held her and by his expression and the tender smile that even now hovered on his lips. He would be honest with Olga, confessing that he now realized he still cared for his first love. Olga would be furious, which was understandable, but she would at the same time be philosophical about the whole affair, realizing that she could not keep Wade to his promise, and that even if she could, there would be no possible chance of happiness for them. 'Lorna. . . .' A shudder passing through his body broke the spell into which she had fallen; an icy finger touched her heart as she was brought from a state of warm ecstatic bliss to a cold sense of reality. Those soaring ideas and confident conclusions had been all her own; she now glanced fearfully up into the face of the man whose hold on her arms was slackening, whose face was an inscrutable mask. 'Forgive me, Lorna. I sincerely apologize for that lapse. It was inexcusable.'

Silence . . . like the hush of doom. A trembling hand stole to her cheek as her face blanched and the ice round her heart gave way to an anguish that was almost physical.

'Lapse. . . .' The word escaped from her quivering lips unintentionally. She stepped back, away from him, and his arms dropped to his sides. 'I'm sorry too,' she continued, a burning heaviness behind her eyes which spread to her temples so that they seared with pain. That she should have stood there, receiving his kisses with such unrestrained eagerness. . . . 'There's nothing to forgive,' she managed in a husky tone, 'it was my fault as much as yours.' She turned away, staring unseeingly at the dark massif engraved against the purple, star-spangled sky. 'We – we should have – have gone in l-long ago—'

Her voice broke and in a fever of haste she made for the archway leading out of the bower. But Wade barred her way, although not intentionally; he just happened to move as if he also would leave this lonely, intimate place. Lorna stopped abruptly and looked up into his face, a plea in her eyes. 'Let me pass,' she murmured, but he stood still.

'I'm sorry,' he said again, taking in the haggard expression, the whiteness of her cheeks. 'I feel a cad, Lorna—' He broke off and she saw a few tiny beads of dampness appear on his forehead. 'Our destinies are not meant to follow one single path,' he added harshly, and turning on his heel he strode away, leaving her to follow, at a much slower pace. But he had not gone far when he turned his head and looked back, just to make sure she was coming. And he waited until she was abreast of him, then matched his pace to hers.

'You have no need to worry,' she assured him tonelessly, 'I shan't go off into the bush again.' She thought he flinched inwardly at her words, because his head jerked and his hand clenched as it swung slightly by his side.

'I'm not afraid of that,' he returned quietly.

'Then please go on. I'd much rather be alone.'

Wade shook his head, keeping his eyes straight in front of him.

'I'll see you into the house.'

Lorna said, after they had been walking for a few moments,

'You'll agree now that I must go from Bali Creek. I hope you'll think of some way to hasten our departure.'

156

He paused in thought. The cry of a dingo once more shattered the silence, which dropped again almost immediately.

'That's going to be difficult,' he began, but Lorna interrupted him, her nerves becoming out of control.

'I'm not staying! I want to go home at once! – just as soon as it can be arranged. You can tell Auntie that you have other visitors coming or that – that as – as your wedding's so close y-you can't be bothered with – with visitors – I don't care what you say to her, but say something that will give her to understand that we're *both* unwelcome – not only me. . . .' Her voice faded, for the words she uttered choked her and articulation became increasingly difficult. Even now she was unable to take it in that Wade could have behaved so callously. Not only had he deliberately hurt her, but by the same act he had been unfaithful to his fiancée.

'Not only you?' He stopped in his tracks as he turned towards her. 'What do you mean?' he demanded to know, and only then did it strike Lorna just what she had revealed.

'It doesn't matter,' she answered impatiently, and would have walked on, but his grip on her wrist halted her.

'You mentioned the word unwelcome. Why?' His face was rather drawn as she looked into it. For one fleeting moment she felt an urge to spare him embarrassment, but that moment passed and as a great wave of bitterness swept over her she did not hesitate to repeat what she had overheard, right at the start, so soon after their arrival at Bali Creek. And this time she was quite sure he flinched inwardly, and two drifts of crimson colour slid up the sides of his mouth. He was sorry . . . sorry for hurting her feelings. Lorna felt in this moment of bitterness and disillusionment that she

157

hated Wade and before he could voice whatever he meant to say by way of apology and contrition she had flashed at him,

'I don't need your pity! Keep it! You've been pitying me for some time – I've seen it,' she snapped as he would have interrupted, 'on so many occasions! I'm not a fool, Wade. I know pity when I see it!'

His eyes glinted suddenly; he was resentful of this onslaught. Lorna sensed that he was hurt too and that it was his intention emphatically to deny her accusation, but all at once his expression changed as anger took possession of him.

'You're obviously trying to make me feel a heel, but before you begin blaming me look back at what you did to me! You threw me over, remember! And now, I suppose, you expect me to throw Olga over just as easily and callously! Well, you can think again— No, don't deny it! I know exactly what you had in mind! *You* might not care how much you hurt people, but I do! So you can put the idea of my jilting Olga right out of your mind!'

She stared at him, into a face pale with fury. And she knew without a shadow of doubt that Wade still loved her. What he had just uttered had been disjointed, to say the least, and it was also inconsistent. He had said that she might not care how much she hurt people, but he did. And yet he was going out of his way to hurt – to hurt her for what she had done to him, for ruining his life – because he knew that if he married Olga his life would without doubt be ruined.

He was striding along again and she skipped a little to keep up with him. She saw now that her conclusions about his pitying her had been all wrong; it was love and love alone that had prompted his kindnesses. How stupid she had been! With a great shuddering sigh she

158

owned to herself that in all her dealings with Wade she had been stupid.

And because of her stupidity happiness was denied both of them, since she was certain that he would never jilt his fiancée. She said, speaking her thoughts aloud,

'You're saying this – about not – er – jilting Olga, but you expected me to jilt my fiancé.'

He stopped, and glowered down at her.

'That was different—'

'Different?'

'Yes, different! You promised me faithfully you would marry me and then went back on your word—'

'Because of Jack's accident,' she cried, wringing her hands. 'You won't try to understand.'

Tossing her plea on one side, he said,

'There's a very great difference. I made you no promise, so I'm not breaking my word. That's the difference!'

Lorna said gently,

'You're splitting hairs, Wade— No, please don't interrupt. I don't expect you to throw Olga over—'

'You did expect it; I saw it in your face.'

She nodded in agreement, but went on to say that she did not now expect him to break his engagement.

'It's a matter of your honour, I understand that now,' she added in the same gentle tones, and she could have gone on to point out that he had not been willing to make the same concession in her case, when he firmly ordered her to break her own engagement. His fierce demanding love at that time had blinded him to everything except the urgent desire to make her his wife. 'As you've said, Wade, our destinies are not meant to follow one single path. Our paths are divided

159

and I accept the entire blame—' A timid hand stole to his sleeve. 'But, Wade, if you could bring yourself to forgive me, then my life would be much more bearable.'

His expression underwent no change whatsoever. It was as uncompromising as his voice when at last he spoke.

'I'll never forgive you – never!'

CHAPTER TEN

THAT he was embittered was plain; that he regretted his engagement was also plain – Lorna had no doubts at all about these conclusions she had reached.

'I should never have come back into his life,' she said when her aunt, noting that Wade totally ignored Lorna both at breakfast and lunch the following day, asked if she and he had quarrelled. 'Meeting me again has caused an upheaval in his life which, quite naturally, he resents.'

'So you have quarrelled?' Aunt Bertha's watched her face closely, evincing no surprise whatsoever at Lorna's words.

'I suppose you would call it a quarrel,' was the reluctant admission after a small hesitation. 'He can't forgive me for what I did to him.'

'Can't forgive ... how stupid men are!' Aunt Bertha's brow creased in a scowl, but it soon cleared. 'You firmly maintained that you had ceased to care for Wade, but that wasn't true, was it, Lorna?'

Without hesitation Lorna shook her head.

'I said it merely so you wouldn't begin feeling guilty. But you've known almost from the first that I lied, haven't you?' And, when her aunt nodded, 'I could tell – by the subtle hints you made at various times.'

'And he loves you – but you don't need me to tell you that?'

Lorna merely inclined her head. Having lain awake through most of the night she had managed among other things to unravel the mystery of her aunt's strange behaviour, realizing that every move and act had been made with the hope of bringing Wade and Lorna together. Deciding it was unnecessary to conceal her deductions, Lorna spoke of them to her aunt.

'You've hoped, right from the start, to bring Wade round to the idea of giving Olga up and marrying me. You've plotted and manoeuvred in all sorts of ways – leaving us to have breakfast alone, for instance, and leaving us together on other occasions. You told Brock I was heartbroken over the death of Jack, just so he'd be kind, and in this way Wade would be made jealous. You've been optimistic, I know, feeling very satisfied with your efforts because at times it did seem that Wade was becoming jealous of Brock—'

'He was jealous of him, as things have turned out. I knew all along that he loved you, and that occasion when he brought up the past was added proof if I required it. I might as well tell you that I still don't believe he'll marry Olga.'

'He will, Auntie,' with conviction, almost before her aunt had finished speaking. And, when her aunt remained silent, 'You plotted, as I've said, and never for one moment did you give a thought to the fact that I might conclude that any kindnesses Wade extended to me were the result of pity, hence the remark you made about your not taking "that aspect into consideration".'

'How long have you known about my – er – scheming?'

'I fathomed it all out last night in bed.'

'You were awake?'

'I couldn't sleep,' Lorna admitted, and hoped that her aunt would allow the subject to drop. But the old lady was not yet ready to oblige.

'Because of your quarrel?'

'Yes; naturally because of our quarrel.'

Her aunt made a swift angry gesture with her hands.

'Why do people always go out of their way to hurt those they love? Surely he has more sense than to marry that horrid girl!'

'It's a question of honour, Auntie. He'll never jilt her.'

'Honour!' derisively. 'Stubbornness, more like— Sheer, darned obstinacy, which is so like a man!'

'He wouldn't spoil his life just because of obstinacy.' Lorna shook her head. 'No, it's honour. In any case, have you thought just how he would be placed were he to break with Olga and marry me? He's a respected member of this Outback community; Olga's parents are his nearest neighbours. Think of the embarrassment and loss of prestige. Everyone would talk about him, he'd be condemned for his action—' Lorna gave another shake of her head. 'He couldn't break his engagement even if he wanted to.' Her aunt said nothing, and after a while Lorna tentatively broached the subject of their going home.

'You want to go soon, naturally.' Her aunt glanced understandingly at her. 'I'm willing to go, dear, just whenever you wish. But I must say that I hate accepting defeat. What a ridiculous situation! You and Wade madly in love and he refusing to break his engagement. It's history repeating itself, but in reverse. You make me so cross, the pair of you! – putting conscience and honour, or whatever you like to call this nonsensical attitude of Wade's, before happiness. You yourself refused to listen to the advice of those who were in a position to view the situation objectively; you just went your own stupid headstrong way with never a thought to the suffering you were inflicting both on yourself and Wade—'

163

'Auntie, we've been through all this before,' broke in Lorna, distressed and on the point of tears. 'Please don't keep reminding me of my mistake.'

'And now Wade,' continued her aunt, disregarding the interruption. 'You'd think a man of his age and intelligence would have more sense than to throw his whole life's happiness away! I hope he regrets it every single second of his life!'

'Auntie! How spiteful of you. Apart from the – the love aspect,' Lorna went on haltingly, 'he and Olga are eminently suited. They belong to the same set; their interests are the same—'

'For goodness' sake, child, don't try my patience any more! Anyone less suited than Olga and Wade I have yet to see! And as for the love aspect, as you call it – well, I'm speechless with amazement.' But apparently she was not speechless at all since she went on and on, ignoring the little protests which Lorna made with her hands. 'Love aspect! You talk as if that's some minor detail to be passed over as if it were neither here nor there. So love doesn't matter, eh? Well, let me tell you, love has been the chief reason for marriage for a very long time, and there's nothing to indicate that it won't be the chief reason for a very long time to come. Do you suppose they can possibly get along without love?'

'If they have other interests,' began Lorna, when she was interrupted once more.

'Do you know what I think? It's just occurred to me that Wade decided to marry in order to have an heir. It would be a natural desire – to wish to have a son. Yes, that's why he got engaged to that girl.' Aunt Bertha fell into a thoughtful mood, but presently Lorna said with a hint of impatience,

'I don't see that it matters why he got engaged to

164

Olga, Auntie. The important thing is that he is engaged, and he's intending to marry her.'

It had already occurred to Lorna that the desire for an heir had influenced Wade in deciding to marry. He had waited a long time, and according to Brock had never looked at another girl seriously until, a few months ago, he had at last begun to take notice of Olga. However, this conclusion was kept to herself, as Lorna wished only to put an end to this most painful conversation. Her aunt seemed at last to understand and began talking about the barbecue, to which some graziers and the families were coming from great distances, and staying the night at Bali Creek. Wade's stockmen, including the Aboriginals and their wives, were also invited, so it appeared there would be quite a crowd. Lorna, looking exceedingly pretty despite her pallor, met Wade just as she was leaving the homestead. Expecting him to prefer his own company she stood aside, making a small gesture to indicate that he should precede her. But he stopped, and he seemed quite unable to keep the appreciative light from his eyes as they roamed over her from head to foot.

'Blue suits you,' he murmured, 'especially that particular shade. What do you call it?'

A soft flush rose and a nervous hand swept a few strands of hair unnecessarily from her shoulder.

'Auntie bought the dress for me; she called it periwinkle blue.'

Wade nodded. Casting him a glance from under her lashes, she noted the taut fixed contours of his face and knew that he was forcing himself not to relax too much.

'Yes, that's what I should call it.' His eyes moved to her hair, shining like pure gold, framing a lovely heart-shaped face. 'Come,' he said abruptly, 'we'll walk over

165

together.

Olga was just arriving with her parents and she approached Wade before Lorna had the chance to leave his side. The girl's eyes swept her an insolent glance before settling on Wade's unsmiling face.

'Is anything wrong, darling?' she inquired silkily. 'You look so dreadfully grim.'

He shook his head, mechanically.

'There's nothing wrong, Olga.' He managed a thin smile as his future in-laws came from the car to join him and the two girls. 'Where's Brock?'

'Coming. He wanted to drive on his own, so he's in the ute.'

'Why did he want to drive on his own?' frowned Wade, his glance going to the overlanding car in which only three people had travelled.

'I think he's going to ask you if he can stay the night.' Mr Norville's swift glance at Lorna betrayed his thoughts and she noticed the sudden hardening of Wade's mouth. 'He appears to be rather keen to take Mrs. Trent into town with him when he goes tomorrow— But I shouldn't have mentioned it; he'll ask you himself, when he gets here.'

'It's because of your disappointment the other day,' interposed Olga with a forced smile for Lorna. 'Er – are you fully recovered from your adventure, Mrs. Trent?'

Lorna's eyes sparkled.

'Yes, thank you, Miss Norville,' she replied stiffly. But she turned to Mr. Noville and said more pleasantly, 'I'm very grateful to you for sending your men out to search for me. Thank you – and I'm very sorry for all the trouble I caused.'

He merely nodded in acknowledgment of the humbly-spoken words, but once again his daughter

166

intervened with,

'It's a wonder you didn't know about the dangers of going off alone into the bush, Mrs. Trent. Wade darling, didn't you warn her?'

His eyes glinted with a light that boded ill for his fiancée once he and she found themselves alone.

He was obviously searching for words which would embarrass neither girl, and Lorna generously came to his rescue.

'Wade did warn me, Miss Norville. But I'd gone a long way before I remembered his warning. In fact, I was already lost before I remembered it.'

Olga's eyes opened very wide.

'You disregarded the warning, in fact?'

Lorna coloured up, but before she had time to speak Wade was saying tautly,

'Lorna's explained, Olga, that she forgot my warning. There was no question of her disregarding it. No one in their right mind would be so reckless as you're suggesting.'

There followed a tense moment of silence; Lorna wished fervently that she could make an excuse and escape, but such an action would be more than a little pointed and untactful at this stage.

'I'm sorry, Wade,' offered his fiancée at length, but in an aggrieved tone, and the swift glance she flashed at Lorna was almost venomous. 'It just seemed to me that Mrs. Trent was passing the matter off far too lightly, and I'm sure none of us would want her to get lost again.'

'There's no possibility of my doing that,' Lorna assured her coldly. And she added, before she could check the words, 'I'm not such a fool as to make the same mistake twice.'

It was Olga's turn to colour; Lorna decided that

167

now was the time to make her retreat. She looked up at Wade and, because she was all woman and the urge to give Olga something to worry about was irresistible, she smiled sweetly at him and murmured softly,

'I must go and find Auntie. You will excuse me, Wade, won't you? And thank you for being so very kind and understanding about my getting lost.' She offered a smile and a nod to Olga's parents and then moved away, reddening now that she had time to dwell on what she had said to Wade. He would know what she had been about; the idea of his having this know-ledge became so embarrassing that by the time she met up with her aunt she was squirming inside.

'Is something wrong, child?' Aunt Bertha inquired in some concern. 'Your face is hot – you're not going to have the 'flu, I hope?'

'Nothing like that,' Lorna replied, but then went on to relate the scene that had taken place. 'I was bitchy, wasn't I? And Wade knows I was.'

'He also knows the destestable girl deserved it all,' pronounced Aunt Bertha, looking extremely aggressive despite the very feminine frilly blouse she wore with a long, slim-fitting black skirt. 'I wish I'd been there! I'd have made her wish she'd never spoken to you like that!' A forefinger was wagged near Lorna's face. 'She'll be her own downfall, that one – just you mark my words!' She turned her head, and her expression underwent a miraculous change. 'Ah, Brock, dear boy! I'll leave you with Lorna, if you don't mind.' She leant a little closer to him. 'I think I've got myself a young man,' she added in a roguish whisper, and was gone.

'Well. . . .' Brock stared after her retreating figure. 'Is that right?'

'Of course not—!' But Lorna's voice cut sharply; her gaze was, like Brock's, on her aunt's back. 'It can't be!'

she added to herself, shaking her head in a disbelieving way. 'The doctor. . . .'

'Howard?' Brock gaped at her. 'Your aunt and the doc! Holy smoke, who'd have thought it! Are you sure?'

Lorna frowned in concentration, her discomfiture entirely erased by this incredible possibility.

'They often sit close together, chatting, when we go out on to the verandah for a sundowner . . . and they danced together almost all the time at your shed dance. Do you remember?'

Brock shook his head.

'I'd eyes only for you,' he returned gallantly.

She passed that off, but not before it had forced an unwilling laugh to her lips.

'Do you think he would marry her?' she asked, thoughts rioting in all directions. The house being sold up; she herself having to find another place, where she would live alone. There was no one in England – no one at all. For years she had leaned a little on her aunt, deriving comfort during those trying times when life was such a burden. Her aunt had visited her and Jack regularly despite her dislike of her niece's husband; she would bring serenity into the house even though at times she could not help scolding Jack, endeavouring to bring him round to a more amicable and grateful frame of mind. 'Do you, Brock?' persisted Lorna, the urgency of fear in her voice.

'I can't say, Lorna— How the dickens can I?'

'No, of course you can't.' Her face had lost its colour, but in the dim lights emitted by the lamps in the trees Brock failed to notice this. 'If she does stay here. . . .' She tailed off, her gaze fixed on the man striding towards her aunt. He stopped on reaching her and they spoke to one another. Howard's arm slid across Aunt

Bertha's shoulders and together they strolled to where the food was being cooked.

'Let's go after them and see what we can find out. Your aunt and the doctor! Well, well! Something for the natter session which will last for a lot longer than nine days, that I can tell you. You obviously don't know it, but every middle-aged woman who comes into contact with Howard sets her cap at him, but he's never had time for any of them.' He shook his head. 'I just can't take it in.'

'We could be jumping to conclusions.'

'Very true,' he agreed, but with a note of scepticism in his voice. Lorna felt flat, dejected in very much the same way as she had felt dejected during those dull thankless years that had gone. If she lost her aunt the future would look black indeed. 'Come. . . .' Brock had his hand under her elbow and he guided her among the little knots of people, chatting and socializing, until he and Lorna were standing right behind Howard and Aunt Bertha. Howard had his arm across Aunt Bertha's shoulders still; he spoke quietly and Lorna frowned and stepped back. 'Don't you want to listen?' whispered Brock, and Lorna's frown deepened.

'Certainly not,' she whispered in reply. 'Shall we get something to eat?'

He shrugged, appearing faintly apologetic.

'You're vexed with me?'

'No; but it isn't the thing to listen to other people's conversation.'

'You're quite right.' He paused a moment. 'I thought you wanted to discover whether or not they were serious?' She said nothing, feeling somewhat impatient with Brock. 'If they are serious,' he went on, 'then she would stay here, of course.'

'Naturally. I don't suppose Howard would want to

170

live in England. Besides, Auntie likes it here; she joked about buying a property.' Lorna moved to where the food was being served, and Brock followed.

'You'd be living alone – if your aunt decided to remain here?'

She nodded, wishing he would change the subject.

'I should have to live alone.'

'You have a home of your own?'

'I told you I lived with my aunt.'

'Yes – but didn't you have a home of your own when you were married?'

She stopped to help herself to a lamb cutlet. Brock stood, undecided, then he also took a cutlet.

'I gave up my home on my husband's death,' she informed Brock at last, and sat down on a long wooden seat which had been placed under a tree. She chose the very end, away from others occupying the centre and who were chatting noisily together. Brock took a seat beside her and began nibbling at his chop.

'So when you return you'll have no home – that is, should your aunt decide to stay here?'

Lorna turned to him, and gave him a frowning glance.

'Just where is this conversation leading?' she asked pointedly, and Brock gave a small start.

'I don't know what you mean, Lorna?'

'You do,' she responded quietly. And when he remained silent she added, 'I'm quite sure you have some idea at the back of your mind, Brock.'

'I see. . . . So you know what I'm getting at?' His face was firm and darkly etched against the firelight. 'I like you a lot,' he managed after a pause. 'I was leading up to a proposal of marriage.'

She wondered how to deal with this without hurting

his pride. His feelings? They could not be hurt for the simple reason that he did not love her. He thought he did, of course, but Lorna at this present time knew him better than he knew himself.

'I'm honoured, Brock,' she said at last in gentle tones, 'but I can't marry you—'

'Why, Lorna? You like me, surely?'

'Liking isn't sufficient,' she told him in the same gentle voice.

'But you can't live all by yourself,' he protested. 'Think about it, Lorna. Please promise me you will?'

She shook her head.

'You're sorry for me,' she stated bitterly. 'I don't want your pity, Brock. As for this talk about my living alone – it's a bit early to make assumptions. Auntie has given me no hint at all that she and the doctor might be serious about each other.'

'So you won't even consider marrying me?' He was downcast, no mistake about that, but Lorna knew no pangs of conscience; he would get over the whole thing in less than a week.

'Marriage isn't in my plans for the future,' she told him, and as at that moment Olga and Wade appeared the subject was dropped.

'Have you arranged your trip to Yarralinga?' Olga inquired languidly of her brother, who frowned darkly at her.

'No; we're not going,' he snapped, and a look of keen satisfaction settled on his sister's face.

Wade looked hard at Lorna, who lowered her eyes under his intense scrutiny.

'You don't want to go into town?' he asked her curiously.

'Brock didn't get down to asking me.'

'No?' Wade's eyes flickered to Brock, who was now

172

actually scowling. Lorna held her breath as she watched his face. There was a short electric silence and then, explosively,

'No! I asked her to marry me instead – and was refused!' And with that he rose from his seat beside her and stalked away, into the darkness.

'He asked you to marry him?' from Olga in tones of amazement and acute distaste. 'I'm very glad you showed sufficient common sense to refuse him, Mrs. Trent—' She was cut off, not by the sudden sparkle appearing in Lorna's eye, but by the look which her fiancé flashed at her. She was certainly asking for trouble, thought Lorna. And Olga herself must have thought so too, because she hurried on, her words running into one another as she endeavoured to detract from her lack of diplomacy in speaking in that manner to a girl who was Wade's guest, 'What I meant was, Brock is at that stage when he's thinking of an heir, and I'm sure you wouldn't want to become his wife merely for that reason. . . .' This time she allowed her voice to tail off more slowly as she realized she had not made a very good job of rectifying her mistake. Wade's set mouth and taut jawline were what at one time would have sent Lorna's heartbeats all of a quiver as apprehension crept over her. Serve Olga right, she thought. She had asked for any censure she would later receive from her fiancé.

'I think we'll change the subject,' from Wade tersely. 'What shall I get you to eat? – or are you coming to choose your own?' He glanced at the cutlet on Lorna's plate. 'Can you recommend those?' His eyes flickered to her face and she nodded.

'This is delicious.' The awkwardness was not passed, despite this casual talk about the food. Olga was livid, because of her own mistakes and the looks which her

173

fiancé had directed at her. She had run headlong into danger, but it was entirely her own fault. It amazed Lorna that she knew so little of Wade's character; she should have been more guarded even before his darkling glance had put an abrupt brake on what she was saying.

'You can get me something, Wade.' Olga smiled up at him in an attempt to bring a softer light to his eyes. She failed and bit her lip in consequence. 'I'll have a cutlet and a hamburger, if you don't mind bringing them for me?'

Without a word he moved away, his figure impressive even among a throng as distinguished-looking as this. Several people spoke to him as he passed them, and once or twice he stopped for a moment or two to converse. Olga sat down, and after a small silence during which Lorna fervently wished she could get away, she said, in those silky tones that seemed to vibrate with insincerity,

'I'm sorry, Mrs. Trent, if I offended you just now. But I was only trying to be helpful. You see, the life here in the Outback can be exceedingly dull for those who, like you, have lived where entertainments and other amenities are taken for granted. Believe me, you'd never have adapted yourself to the change of environment.'

Without turning her head Lorna said quietly,

'I had no intention of accepting your brother's offer, Miss Norville, so you needn't have been so concerned. I don't love him and he doesn't care for me in that way.'

'Love. . . .' The girl dwelt for some time on this one short word after uttering it. She said, slowly and maliciously, 'You're probably in love with someone else, Mrs. Trent?'

Lorna glanced up from her plate, her nerves tensed. If only Wade would come back. . . .

'I don't think I understand,' she parried, but the other girl uttered a swift impatient exclamation that cut short anything else Lorna would have found to say.

'It isn't difficult to see that you have a crush on Wade. I should imagine everyone has noticed it.'

A hush fell. Lorna wondered what Olga would say were she to inform her that this speciousness was wasted as she, Lorna, was in possession of the fact that Olga had uttered these words only on the basis of her prior knowledge – knowledge gained when she had deliberately taken a snapshot from Wade's pocket. But of course Lorna could not have divulged her own knowledge even had she wanted to, since it would mean giving Brock away. A deep flush had risen to cover Lorna's cheeks and without thinking she glanced up as Wade returned carrying two plates and two paper napkins. He stopped abruptly, his flickering eyes moving several times from one girl to the other. Lorna gave a sigh, relieved to have escaped the necessity of finding a response to the other girl's detestable words.

'Shall I sit here?' Wade's voice, polite but so cold that Lorna shuddered involuntarily. He was about to sit between them, but Olga moved up, closer to Lorna, and so he took the space at his fiancée's side.

'Thank you, darling.' She accepted the plate offered, and flipped the napkin from his fingers with a dainty gesture. A smile broke, dazzlingly, and Lorna had the strange sensation that the smile was in effect an arrogant command for him to let fall his cold exterior and treat her as a fiancée should be treated. If Wade had the same impression he kept it concealed beneath the unchanging mask, and his voice remained coldly polite as he replied to Olga's casually-spoken questions. The atmosphere all round was too intense for comfort and presently Lorna found an excuse to leave the couple on their own.

She caught up with her aunt and Howard and they chatted for a while. Aunt Bertha eventually asked where Brock was and Lorna went quiet for a space.

'He's gone off somewhere,' she replied casually at last.

'Where, dear?' Aunt Bertha's eyes wandered all around. 'I don't see him.'

'You won't, in all that crowd.'

Her aunt looked searchingly at her.

'You sound tired, dear,' she remarked tactfully. 'I shouldn't stay out too long.'

'No, I think I'll go in quite soon.' Lorna was dispirited, not only as a result of her own feelings but also by the thought of Wade's marrying anyone so detestable as Olga. How had he come to ask her to marry him in the first place? she wondered. But then she admitted that the girl could appear most charming if she so desired.

'Perhaps you haven't quite recovered from your ordeal out there in the bush,' suggested the doctor, eyeing her face critically. 'Yes, I should have an early night if I were you.'

She nodded absently, her attention with her aunt. But there was nothing to be read in her expression and after a while Lorna left them and wended her way through the laughing, chatting throng of graziers and their families and employees, hoping to reach the homestead unobserved. No one would miss her once she was gone, she thought, frowning as Robert and the two students joined her. They all stopped and chatted

176

and a short time later Howard joined the group. Automatically Lorna looked around for her aunt, but before she could voice the question rising to her lips Howard asked if he could speak to her privately.

'Of course.' She knew at once why he had come. Her glance flickered to the others in turn and they obligingly moved away. 'What is it, doctor?'

He began to speak; Lorna learned that he and her aunt wanted to marry, but her aunt absolutely refused to abandon her niece. She could not live all alone, Aunt Bertha had said.

'And so she won't marry me – even though she admits she would like to,' Howard continued frowningly. 'I said you could have a home with us, but she seems certain you'd refuse. That's why I had to speak to you myself, because there appears to be some mystery. You like it here; you've fitted into the life splendidly, so why should she be sure you'll refuse my offer?' He paused a moment. 'Is there any special reason why you can't make your home with us?'

Lorna was thoughtful. She would love to settle here, but not as the doctor's guest. She must pay her way, and there was no job for her at Bali Creek. In any case, it was unthinkable that she could remain once Olga and Wade were married. The doctor was repeating his question and Lorna was obliged to answer.

'There is a reason,' she admitted, but immediately went on to add, 'However, it mustn't affect you and Auntie. I want her to be happy; she mustn't sacrifice herself for me. I'll talk to her about this matter,' Lorna promised finally.

'I'm afraid your aunt will be vexed with me if you do,' he began uneasily. 'She forbade me to tackle you. Just now I managed to leave our little group unnoticed, and came to seek you out, but—' He stopped, frowning.

177

'No, you mustn't say anything to her.'

'I'll be diplomatic,' she assured him with a smile. 'As a matter of fact I'd already begun to suspect a romance—'

'You had?'

'It wasn't surprising, really. You and she, sitting close on the verandah, and this evening – you were strolling about with your arm around her shoulders.'

'Yes . . . yes, I suppose it must have been there for anyone to see.'

'So I can speak to her without mentioning this little talk we've had,' Lorna continued, picking up from where the interruption had occurred. 'Don't worry, everything will be all right.'

'Thank you, dear.'

'You had better go back,' she advised. 'Auntie mustn't see us together.'

She stood there a moment, her eyes on his retreating figure. She was glad for her aunt, and sincerely hoped she would be successful in influencing her to marry the doctor.

Turning presently, Lorna began once again to proceed towards the homestead, keeping to the edge of a small clump of coolibah trees in order to take advantage of the shadows offered. Suddenly she came to a halt, instinctively pressing against the trunk of a tree as she heard voices. Wade and Olga. . . . How stupid of her to stop, Lorna chided herself, wondering how she was to escape unseen by the couple, who were also in the shadows, but very close to where she stood hidden by the tree.

'—shall not be subjected to the indignity of being made to look small before that girl—!'

'You asked for it – and on more than one occasion! What reason have you for disliking her? Right at the

178

beginning ,you lied in order to cause a misunderstanding between Lorna and me.'

A quarred. . . . Heart pounding, Lorna glanced around with a sort of urgent desperation. She must get away, for she had no wish to eavesdrop on a quarrel between Wade and his fiancée. Yet if she were to move now they must surely see her.

'Why didn't I think before I stopped?' she asked herself exasperatedly.

'You told me over the air that the girl who was coming was a friend,' rasped Olga, ignoring his question and statement. 'But she was more than a friend, wasn't she?'

Lorna gasped. Did Olga realize just what she had done?

'More . . .?' So soft the tone, but in the clarity of the arid air it came quite plainly to Lorna. It carried a menacing note and involuntarily she shivered. Wade was in an ugly mood, that was for sure. 'And how, might I ask, did you acquire that knowledge?'

'So you admit it?' Olga's voice quivered slightly; she was playing for time – or perhaps hoping for a diversion, so that she could escape an answer to Wade's question. Automatically Lorna was shaking her head, silently telling Olga that it was no use. If Wade desired to know more then he would most certainly force the truth from her.

'I admit it,' from Wade firmly but in the same misleadingly quiet voice.

'And do you admit that you still love her?' Olga's rising tones were fringed with something akin to venom. 'Do you?'

No answer. After a small intense silence Wade repeated his question.

'You might as well tell me how you came by the

179

knowledge,' he added, 'because I mean to have the truth.'

Again his fiancée tried to divert him.

'It seems to me,' she said, 'that you're wanting to end our engagement?' A pause for Wade to speak, but he remained silent. Lorna edged softly to the next tree, a little farther away from the couple whose quarrel she was reluctantly being forced to overhear. She held her breath for a moment after moving, but then breathed freely again. They had not seen her. If she could manage to dodge to the next tree, and the one after that, then she could probably walk away. 'I'll never let you end it!' Olga was saying raspishly. 'I'm not losing face, so you can put any ideas of a broken engagement right out of your head!'

Another gasp as Lorna heard this. Olga was certainly heading for trouble. But whatever Wade's inner reaction to the outburst all he said was,

'I'm still waiting for an answer to my question, Olga.'

The girl began speaking, disjointedly, her voice becoming a harsh crescendo of fury, and Lorna seized the opportunity of stealing softly to the next tree. A third was reached and with a sigh of relief she was able to leave the shadows and stroll along naturally. But of course she arrived back where she started from and was just debating on taking one of the other paths when bedlam seemed to be let loose.

'One of the brumbies!' a man's voice shouted as everyone scattered at the sound of thudding hooves. 'It's broken out of the paddock!'

A dozen warning shouts sounded in Lorna's ears, but her legs were paralysed. The horse thundered towards her, mane flying as its magnificent head tossed, nostrils flaring. She was right in its path and the warning cries

180

became louder and more urgent. The thudding almost deafened her, but through it she heard Wade's voice, strangled, commanding, as he raced alongside the spellbound crowd.

'Lorna – for God's sake move!' But she remained rooted to the spot, her heart hammering, her mind and body numbed with terror. 'Lorna—' She was conscious of a searing pain as a hoof caught her temple and with a little moan she waited for the agony of being trampled beneath those stampeding feet. But the brumbie's wildly-flowing mane was grasped and with what must have been superhuman strength Wade swung the horse round with no more than a second to spare. 'Lorna . . . my love. . . .' She felt him pick her up from where she had fallen, vaguely aware that several of the stockmen had sped up to tackle the brumbie and return it to the paddock. People talking all at once . . . someone praising Wade's swiftness of action . . . a voice saying it was a miracle she was alive . . . another, harsh and cracked,

'The stupid girl! She had plenty of time to get out of its way!'

Olga. . . .

'I'm so sorry, Wade—' Lorna's voice was husky with pain. 'I tried to move – really I did, but I was just stricken with – with terror.'

'Hush, my darling, hush.' He was carrying her so easily. She dropped her head against his shoulder and thought to herself,

'I shouldn't; the blood will spoil his clothes.'

'Lorna! Lorna, oh, my child, are you all right?' Aunt Bertha, with the doctor, trotting alongside Wade as he strode towards the homestead.

'Yes, Auntie; there's no need to worry.'

'If it hadn't been for Wade's timely action—' Aunt

181

Bertha stopped, unable to finish the sentence.

Howard followed as after entering the house Wade took Lorna up to her bedroom and gently laid her down on the bed. After a brief examination Howard straightened up, satisfied.

'A nasty wound, but nothing serious.' He looked down at her. 'You're just about the luckiest person around these parts,' he told her.

One of the lubras had been sent off for hot water, and quite soon Lorna was sitting on the bed, the wound cleansed and dressed. Wade stood by the bed and watched the entire operation, and when the doctor had gone – literally tugged away by Aunt Bertha, whose face wore a most satisfied smile – he sat down on a chair and opened his mouth to say something, but he was interrupted by a tap on the bedroom door.

'Miss Norville wishes to speak to you, Boss.' Dinah looked curiously at him. 'She says at once.'

Wade rose, eyes glinting dangerously.

'Where is she?'

'In the living-room.' Wade nodded a dismissal, following closely as the girl left the room. Less than five minutes later he was back, a smile instantly softening his features as his eyes met those of Lorna. She had slid from the bed and was standing before the long mirror surveying the large white dresssing which covered the nasty gash she had received from the horse's hoof. She turned right round after holding his gaze through the mirror – turned with compulsion, and yet she was shy and awkward and she almost wished he had not returned quite so quickly. Her long lashes came down, hiding her expression. She was under a great stress of uncertainty; she dared not voice the question hovering on her lips. With infinite understanding Wade covered the separating distance and without a word enfolded her in his arms. He bent to kiss her, with such great tenderness, and his heartbeats raced as rapidly as her own.

'It's all right, my dearest,' he murmured at last, his mouth against her cheek. 'Everything's all right now.'

'All right. . . .' It wasn't true, it could not be. . . . She trembled against him, then nestled more closely to his heart, for reassurance. 'Olga . . .?'

He began to tell Lorna of the quarrel, but without entering into details. As Lorna had known, he had forced the truth from Olga; he knew she had overheard what he said to his mother and he also knew of course of her deplorable action in going into his pocket for the snapshot.

'I was too disgusted for speech—' His underlip rolled with contempt as he dwelt for a moment on Olga's conduct in taking something from his coat pocket. 'I told her our engagement was at an end.' He stopped and Lorna saw that he would rather have left everything unsaid. But there was much to explain and he went on, 'There never was any love on either side; it was to be a marriage of convenience – suitable for two people who had certain desires but who could never give one another love. My desire was to have an heir, Olga's the status which marriage would provide. She has position and wealth; she had no intention of marrying anyone who couldn't provide her with what she had been used to. I fitted into her scheme of things and she fitted into mine. I'd never have married a girl I could hurt; and as I loved you, and always would, I had no love to give anyone else. That was why I chose Olga, but also, as she was the exact opposite to you, I was safeguarded as to the danger of ever being reminded of you.'

183

'Auntie came to that very conclusion.' Lorna spoke quickly, trying to keep back the tears which emotion was bringing to her eyes. That Wade should have loved her all this time . . . and that he should be able to say with such confidence that he would always love her. 'You – you make me f-feel so s-sad. . . .' She hadn't intended saying anything like that; it slipped out unbidden, and because he understood how she felt he drew her close and, tilting her face, he pressed his tender lips to hers.

'I know I said dreadful things to you in my anger,' he owned contritely after a long while, 'but, dearest, I never meant them – not in my heart.' He shuddered – so unlike him, she thought, because it seemed in some way to be at variance with his great strength. 'My beloved . . . it's been such a long, long time . . . an eternity.' His lips found hers again and it seemed he would never draw them away. 'My own, at last. It's a miracle!'

She thought, 'I was an unwelcome guest on my arrival,' and aloud she said,

'It is indeed a miracle.'

Wade accurately read her thoughts and his contrition returned.

'To think that I didn't want you here! You see, darling, I felt that there was nothing to be gained by opening up old wounds, for at that time I was content with the bargain I'd made with Olga. Also, I couldn't see myself jilting her— Yes, my love, I know I made no concessions when you refused to jilt Jack, but I understand now, for honour prevailed with me just as it had with you. Even when I felt I couldn't live without you – and I have felt that way almost since the day you came back into my life – I couldn't bring myself even to think of letting Olga down. You see, at that time I had no excuse for doing so. But when I learned of her disgusting act in going into my pocket, and when I saw her with you and realized she possessed an altogether different side to her nature, then I knew I had reason to reconsider. She firmly said she wasn't having the humiliation of a broken engagement, but I was adamant. However, she's just asked me if she can let it be known that *she* has thrown *me* over. That's what she wanted to see me for just now. I agreed, naturally.'

A deep silence followed and after a little while Lorna lifted her face, pleading for a kiss. His eyes lit with tender emotion as he bent his head.

'You dear sweet child; you haven't changed one scrap. I adore you, Lorna!' He felt her heart throbbing joyously against him as his lips came, warm and tender, to meet hers. 'I hated Brock,' he said as if a pang of jealousy even now shot through him. 'I hated him even though I knew you'd never consent to marry him, because it was me you loved.'

She leant away and looked up into his eyes.

'Auntie,' she began, and went on to tell him everything she had deduced that night when she lay awake in bed.

'The sly old schemer!' he ejaculated. 'What a lot of heartache she caused me!'

'That was the idea,' laughed Lorna. 'She told Brock a sob story about my being heartbroken over Jack's death, so that Brock would be sorry for me and fuss me, as it were. That would make you jealous, and once you were jealous you'd begin to think about jilting Olga and marrying me. She had it worked out beautifully – but when you began being kind to me I suddenly concluded that it was pity—' Lorna broke off and pressed against him. 'I – I just couldn't bear it,' she quivered, 'my having your pity while Olga had your love. That

185

was why I became cool with you, but I had difficulty in keeping it up.'

'So that was the reason for the change? Pity?' He shook his head. 'It was always love, my dearest. Didn't I once say that you and I were meant for one another?'

She nodded dreamily and murmured an agreement.

Wade laughed and drew her close; she stirred contentedly against his breast, her eyes glowing like stars.

'Auntie will be so very pleased. She'll always claim the credit – but then she has a right to claim it.' A small silence. 'That was a lucky win. ... Oh, I completely forgot! Auntie and the doctor are getting married—'

'What?' He held her from him and stared. 'What did you say?'

'It's true.' Lorna went on to explain, while Wade kept shaking his head in disbelief.

'I never thought Howard would ever marry.' He paused in thought. 'It's wonderful news – not that we would have let her go back and live on her own, of course. I intended offering her a home—' He looked lovingly into Lorna's eyes. 'Because I owe her so much,' he added emotionally, 'so very much.'

'We both do,' she agreed fervently. 'It's fitting that she too is going to be happy.'

Another silence ensued and when it ended Lorna's lips and cheeks were rosy from his lovemaking.

'I'll give you that trip to Alice – for your honeymoon,' he said, and immediately added, 'You'll marry me at once?' Although phrased as a request it was in fact an order.

'But of course,' she returned obligingly, still rather stunned by all that was happening to her. 'Whatever you say, darling.'

'The fourth bride of Bali Creek,' he murmured with tender emotion, his hands closing about her slender waist, 'and the best loved of them all....'

Attention: Harlequin Collectors!

of Harlequin Romances now available

We are proud to present a collection of the best-selling Harlequin Romances of recent years. This is a unique offer of 100 classics, lovingly reissued with beautifully designed new covers. No changes have been made to the original text. And the cost is only 95¢ each.

Not sold in stores, this series is available only from Harlequin Reader Service.

Send for FREE catalog!

Harlequin Reader Service
MPO Box 707,
Niagara Falls, N.Y. 14302

In Canada:
Stratford, Ontario
N5A 6W4

Please send me my free Harlequin Collection catalog.

NAME_____

ADDRESS _____

CITY _____

STATE/PROV._____ ZIP/POSTAL CODE_____

OFFER EXPIRES DECEMBER 31, 1977   MOR 2099

Have you missed any of these best-selling Harlequin Romances?

By popular demand...
to help complete your collection of Harlequin Romances

50 titles listed on the following pages...

Harlequin Reissues

1282 **The Shining Star**
Hilary Wilde

1284 **Only My Heart to Give**
Nan Asquith

1285 **Out of a Dream**
Jean Curtis

1288 **The Last of the Kintyres**
Catherine Airlie

1289 **The Much-Loved Nurse**
Pauline Ash

1292 **Falcon's Keep**
Henrietta Reid

1293 **I Know My Love**
Sara Seale

1294 **The Breadth of Heaven**
Rosemary Pollock

1295 **Suddenly It Was Spring**
Hilda Pressley

1353 **Nurse Lavinia's Mistake**
Marjorie Norrell

1363 **Star Dust**
Margaret Malcolm

1365 **Hotel Southerly**
Joyce Dingwell

1368 **Music I Heard with You**
Elizabeth Hoy

1371 **Dancing on My Heart**
Belinda Dell

1372 **Isle of Pomegranates**
Iris Danbury

1384 **Beloved Enemies**
Pamela Kent

1390 **Sugar in the Morning**
Isobel Chace

1394 **Nurse Sandra's Second Summer**
Louise Ellis

1397 **If Love Were Wise**
Elizabeth Hoy

1433 **The Pursuit of Dr. Lloyd**
Marjorie Norrell

1435 **Scarlet Sunset**
Mary Cummins

1439 **Serenade at Santa Rosa**
Iris Danbury

1440 **Bleak Heritage**
Jean S. MacLeod

1444 **Fond Deceiver**
Pauline Garnar

1449 **Dedication Jones**
Kate Norway

Harlequin Reissues

Complete and mail this coupon today!

Harlequin Reader Service
MPO Box 707
Niagara Falls, N.Y. 14302

In Canada:
Harlequin Reader Service
Stratford, Ontario N5A 6W4

Please send me the following Harlequin Romances. I am enclosing my check or money order for 95¢ for each novel ordered, plus 25¢ to cover postage and handling.

☐ 1282	☐ 1394	☐ 1481
☐ 1284	☐ 1397	☐ 1483
☐ 1285	☐ 1433	☐ 1484
☐ 1288	☐ 1435	☐ 1638
☐ 1289	☐ 1439	☐ 1643
☐ 1292	☐ 1440	☐ 1647
☐ 1293	☐ 1444	☐ 1651
☐ 1294	☐ 1449	☐ 1652
☐ 1295	☐ 1456	☐ 1654
☐ 1353	☐ 1457	☐ 1659
☐ 1363	☐ 1462	☐ 1675
☐ 1365	☐ 1464	☐ 1677
☐ 1368	☐ 1468	☐ 1686
☐ 1371	☐ 1473	☐ 1691
☐ 1372	☐ 1475	☐ 1695
☐ 1384	☐ 1477	☐ 1697
☐ 1390	☐ 1478	

Number of novels checked _____ @ 95¢ each = $_____

N.Y. and N.J. residents add appropriate sales tax $_____

Postage and handling $_____.25

TOTAL $_____

NAME _____
(Please print)

ADDRESS _____

CITY _____

STATE/PROV. _____ ZIP/POSTAL CODE _____

MOR 2099